UNTIL
THE OCEAN
FREEZES

All the best
Simone! Enjoy
the book.

-Alida

UNTIL THE OCEAN FREEZES

Alida Durham Clemans

Until the Ocean Freezes
Copyright © 2020 by Alida Durham Clemans

Cover art copyright © 2020 by Lisa Myers

Interior art copyright © 2020 by Shantih E. Clemans
and Chloe Clemans Shapiro

Cover design by Aoife Leonard

Visit the author's website: www.alidadurhamclemans.com

ISBN: 9781081731410

Published by 15th Street Books

Printed in the United States of America
by Kindle Direct Publishing

For Marc, Zoe & Lucas

Chapter 1

"Ms. Olsen is the meanest teacher ever!" the girl next to Lizzy whispered. They were sitting along the edge of the pool, dangling their feet into the cold water.

"She is?" Lizzy whispered back.

"Yup, but she likes me," said the girl. Her skin was the color of coffee ice cream, and her curly black hair was braided in neat sections all over her head and tied with red and yellow rubber bands.

Lizzy didn't know what to say. She guessed everyone in the class was probably around her age, although they were a mix of heights and sizes. As usual, Lizzy was one of the tallest.

"Listen up, people. We're going to get started. No more talking," the teacher's commanding voice punctuated the hot air of the pool deck. With short brown hair and thick eyebrows, she looked younger than Lizzy's mom. Her uniform consisted of gray gym shorts over a dark-green one-piece suit and flip-flops. An official-looking red whistle hung around her neck.

After Lizzy and the other kids put on their swim caps (which the Y required), some girls struggling to tuck in their hair, the students were instructed to line up along the blue-tiled wall.

"Today we are going to work on our dives. Form three lines and let's see what you can do," barked Ms. Olsen.

Lizzy had never learned to dive properly. Now she was about to embarrass herself in front of all these strangers. She wanted to disappear down the drain.

The girl who'd just spoken, who wore an orange and purple swimsuit with an explosion of white stars across the front and a white swim cap, was on the line next to Lizzy.

"Miss Reed, can you demonstrate for your fellow swimmers?" asked the teacher, directing her attention to the girl with the star suit. As the rest of the class watched, she executed a perfect dive, her compact body slicing into the water like an acrobat.

"That's how it's done," Ms. Olsen announced as Miss Reed pulled herself out of the water. Lizzy hated her already.

Ms. Olsen blew her whistle. "Okay, swimmers, let's dive. You three go first," she said, motioning to the two girls and one boy at the front of the three lines. The boy sneezed. Maybe he was allergic to chlorine.

"Remember, curl your toes around the lip of the pool, tuck your head between your arms, bend your knees and spring forward." She made it sound so easy.

One after the other, the kids attempted their dives. Some were better than others, but they were all way better than Lizzy could ever hope to be. Maybe kids in New York City were born knowing how to swim and dive.

When her turn came, Lizzy tried to remember what her teacher had told them—curl toes, tuck head, bend knees, and jump—but she fell clumsily into the pool, making a messy splash. Feeling her face redden, she ducked under the water to escape. Class couldn't end soon enough.

Chapter 2

"Can you give me a hand, honey?" Lizzy's mother, Margot, asked.

She was pulling bubble wrap off dishes and arranging them in the just-washed cabinet above the sink.

Hair still wet from the shower, Lizzy put down her book and came over to help. She reached into a box on the floor and pulled out a small bundle. "Oh, here are my buddies!" she exclaimed, ripping the newspaper to reveal her favorite salt-and-pepper shakers, the ones shaped like Westie dogs.

"Let's leave them out, to keep an eye on you," said her mom with a wink.

She placed the ceramic figurines on the countertop, next to the coffee maker and the blender used to make Lizzy's dad's protein smoothies, which smelled like gym socks but were supposedly good for him.

"So how was swim class? Daddy said you were quiet on the way home," her mom asked as she collected a pile of bubble wrap and began to stuff it into a white garbage bag.

It had only been three days since the movers packed up her yellow house in New Jersey after the last day of fifth grade and brought everything in a big truck to this apartment.

Their things were still in the middle of being unpacked. Although most of the furniture was arranged, boxes and balled-up paper were everywhere, and framed artwork leaned against the wall. Lizzy's room was a total disaster.

"I don't want to talk about it. I just want to move back to our old house."

"I know this is hard, but we can't move back," said her mother. "I'm about to start my new job. And living here is better for Dad. We've been over this, sweetheart."

She crossed her arms over her chest and stared at her mother. "Dad's fine. He doesn't even seem that sick."

"Dad *is* doing well, but you know he has good days and bad days, right? And being close to his doctors makes a lot of sense."

"Okay, but I don't want to take swim lessons, Mom. Why are you making me?"

"Lizzy, I told you, you'll get exercise and meet people," her mother said. "Isn't that a good thing?"

"Why can't I take a drawing class instead?"

"Because there aren't any appropriate art classes at the Y. I'll look for a more advanced class for you somewhere else. Maybe at one of the museums. In the meantime, please do your best. It's important to try things you're not so comfortable doing, like swimming. It builds character."

Just then, Lizzy's dad, Cal, and her little brother, Julian, came in, a pizza box balanced on the handles of the stroller.

"Lizzy! We found an ice cream store! It's called Frosty's!" shouted Julian, interrupting Lizzy's conversation with her mother. "We're going to go after dinner. Daddy said!"

He jumped from his stroller and ran past his father into the kitchen. Penny, the family's scruffy rescue terrier, sprang up from her spot on the couch to greet them. Lizzy grabbed the pizza and put it on the table.

"Here, Jules, have a drink," said their mom, filling his sippy cup with cold water from the faucet.

Julian, who just turned three, had dark hair and the bright blue eyes of a husky. They were that blue. His coloring was like their dad's, except his eyes were lighter. Chances were good that he could end up with his father's big nose, but it was too early to know for sure.

For now, Julian's nose was an adorable button in the middle of his round face, and he had pink cheeks and the softest skin Lizzy had ever felt, almost as soft as the fur on Penny's belly that she loved to have rubbed.

Lizzy's eyes were green, like her mom's, and she had pale skin and way too many freckles. Her hair fell in messy waves around her face. Most days, she tied the loose pieces back with a clip.

Instead of forgettable brown, Lizzy's red hair was so vibrant it made it hard for her to hide in the back of a classroom or walk down the street unnoticed. Everyone noticed redheads.

But back in Mount Olive, Lizzy was just one of the girls in fifth grade. Even with her hair, she felt like she fit right in. She missed her old friends so much. Being with them was always easy.

She never had to think about what to say or what to do. It just happened. She wondered what Hannah and Amy were up right now.

Subject : Hi!
From : elizamurphyzander@gmail.com
To : amyyvonnekim@gmail.com

Dear Amy,

I am going to alternate writing to you and Hannah. I wrote both your names on pieces of paper and folded them up into little squares. Then I made Julian pick one out of my breakfast bowl (that was <u>before</u> I poured in my corn flakes and milk, don't worry!)—and it was you! I guess you had a 50% chance so it's not all that amazing. Anyway, I'm writing to you first. I'll write to Hannah next, probably tomorrow since I'll have nothing better to do.

First of all, I HATE IT HERE!!! It's going to be the worst summer ever!!! I want to move back to Mount Olive. You would not believe how small my room is. I have barely enough space to fit my little bed and my dresser. I put my stand-up mirror on top with my pink hairbrush, my Lip Smackers (Bubblegum flavor!) and my asthma pump.

NYC already makes me wheeze. I don't have a closet or a desk. My mom thinks I'll be fine doing my homework on the dining table by the front door (we have no dining room!!!), which sounds like the worst place in the world to concentrate. And we all have to share one bathroom!

The city is busy and dirty, and everyone is in a hurry. There are zero houses—just tall buildings and so much construction everywhere! The sidewalks are so hot and the garbage stinks. And there are homeless people begging for money. I feel sorry for them but they kind of scare me too. I miss riding my bike.

On the good side, it is fun to ride the elevator up to our apartment on the fourth floor. I haven't officially met anyone in the building yet, but I've seen a bunch of weird-looking people.

A large dog growled at Penny when we took her out for a walk. She probably still smells like New Jersey. I read somewhere that dogs think with their noses! Isn't that fascinating?!

I wish we were at the Memorial Pool right now. My mom is making me take swimming lessons at the Y. The first class was horrendous (I had to look up how to spell that!). I have to figure out a way to get out of this stupid idea of hers. Maybe I'll get sick or run over by a taxi. I wish she had signed me up for an art class instead. Hey, did your mom take you shopping for a new swimsuit yet? Mine is same old ugly.

I'm still wearing my friendship bracelets. Hope you and Hannah are too! I'm never taking them off!

I gotta go—we're going "exploring"—whatever that means. I miss you a lot. Like so so so much. E-mail me back soon!!!!!!!

Love 'til the ocean freezes,
Me

P.S. BEST FRIENDS 4-Ever!

After dinner and ice cream (a dish of mint-chip for Lizzy and rocky road on a sugar cone with rainbow sprinkles for Julian), Lizzy changed into her polka-dot pajama pants and an old Lincoln Elementary School T-shirt.

Sitting cross-legged on her unmade bed, she unzipped her red L.L. Bean backpack, the one with her initials sewn on the front in white stitching and the tiny rip in the seam that contained her important items.

First, the photo of Hannah and Amy from the Spring Fling that they gave her as a going-away present on their last night together.

The three had, of course, gone to Hill's on Elm Street for milkshakes and French fries with a side of ketchup for dipping.

Lizzy held the acrylic frame in her hands. With her index finger, whose chewed nail was decorated with neon-blue polish, she touched Amy's face, then Hannah's. She remembered that Hannah hadn't smiled that night when her dad shouted, "Say Cheese!" because she was hiding her new braces. They made her self-conscious and her mouth sore.

It was still a great picture. Hannah and Amy were her best friends. She wasn't sure who she was without them.

Next, Lizzy removed her flowered wallet and opened the change purse. Phew, her good-luck charm was safe. She didn't know what she would do if she lost the heart-shaped pendant she'd carried with her for three whole years, especially since luck (the good kind!) was what she needed the most right now.

Inside the wallet was a brand-new twenty-dollar bill Aunt Fiona had given her as an early-early birthday present, even though Lizzy wouldn't be twelve until November.

"Buy something fun," she had said. Lizzy didn't want to spend it right away.
Reaching further into her backpack, Lizzy grabbed a small spiral sketchbook and a rectangular metal box containing twenty-three pencils in every imaginable color (pencil #24, "Arctic Lime," had disappeared in her old room months ago).

She hadn't felt like drawing anything since they moved here. She was just getting around to unpacking her art supplies.

Lizzy wondered whose job it was to name the colors of colored pencils. Maybe

- Lizzy

she could do that when she grew up. If she made it through the summer.

Flipping through her sketchbook, she turned to her drawing of Penny, with her long copper-colored fur (which she hated to have brushed), the one she started when she still lived in Mount Olive. She wished she had the energy to finish it.

Lizzy closed her eyes and took a deep breath. Her mom promised she'd adjust. But what if she never did? What if moving to New York turned out to be the worst idea ever?

Then what?

Chapter 3

Julian had woken up in a cheerful mood. "Hello there, beautiful boy," Margot said. "Did you have a nice nap?" Lizzy couldn't help feeling a little jealous listening to her mom fuss over her brother.

Julian laughed as their mother tickled his ribs and smothered his face with kisses. Lizzy didn't remember being treated that way when she was his age. Even older sisters needed to be babied sometimes. But her mom didn't seem to get that.

After a diaper change, Julian climbed into his stroller, and their mom secured the straps around his shoulders and between his legs.

"Lizzy, come with us. Dad is resting," their mother said as she slipped on Lizzy's brother's white sneakers and handed him Bob the Bunny. He brought that worn-out rabbit with him everywhere.

"You know how stress can exacerbate your dad's condition," she added, lowering her voice to an almost whisper.

Lizzy hated when her mother used words like "exacerbate" and "condition." Why couldn't she talk to her like a normal person?

"Can Penny come?" asked Lizzy, reaching for the orange leash. The dog jumped up and down excitedly.

"Not this time, honey," said her mom. "It's too hot for her, plus we're running errands where dogs may not be allowed. Let her stay with Daddy."

Disappointed, Lizzy held the door open while her mother wheeled Julian out to the elevator. "Bye Dad! Love you!" she shouted into the apartment. She paused

9

for a second but didn't hear an answer. Maybe he was sleeping already. Maybe he was listening to music with his headphones.

"Where are we going, anyway?" Lizzy asked, as she shuffled along sullenly. The afternoon sun heated up the sidewalk. She felt like she was walking into an oven. She took a sip of her water bottle.

"To the library to sign us up for library cards, then to the liquor store for some wine for your father and me," said her mom as she fished her sunglasses out of her purse.

"Wow, that sounds so much more fun than staying inside in the air conditioning."

"Knock it off, Lizzy. I don't appreciate your sarcasm. This move has been hard for all of us, not just you," she snapped.

"Yeah, Lizzy!" Julian chimed in, not sure what he was agreeing to. Lizzy wanted to punch him in the nose.

The public library was in a plain tan building on Twenty-Third Street. Hanging outside the second-story window, a bright orange banner waved in the hot breeze. A silver metal box for book returns sat to the right of the entrance.

Two women and a little girl with red hair were walking out when they got there. Lizzy smiled at her. She always smiled at redheads. After all, they were members of the ginger club, whether they liked it or not.

Stepping inside, Lizzy noticed that the air conditioning didn't seem to be working too well, but it was way better than being outside. Already she was a sweaty mess.

"I'm going upstairs," said Lizzy. "That's where my books are." She followed a sign for the library's middle grade and young adult collections. Her mom, pushing the stroller with Julian, who had fallen asleep, headed over to the desk to inquire about library cards.

Lizzy wandered through the crowded shelves, running her fingers along the spines of each volume. She was looking for a book to read with her dad. They were almost finished with the first book in *The Sisters Grimm* series and needed something new.

She loved listening to her dad's animated voice and imagining herself in a different world. One where she could draw all day long, eat plates of Oreos, and didn't have to go to a new school.

Lizzy collected a stack of books and put them down on a small wooden table. Settling into a brown armchair and resting her feet on the worn-out blue carpet, she examined each book one by one, studying the titles and the cover illustrations and skimming the opening pages. As hard as she tried to focus on the books, her mind wandered. She felt worried about everything.

Before they moved, Lizzy's mom researched all the middle schools in District 2, where they would be living, and filled out an application form listing several possible choices, one of which accepted Lizzy. The system was much more complicated than in Mount Olive, that was for sure!

Lizzy's new school had an awful name. School of Tomorrow sounded like a weird place for aliens or robots, not a plain-old middle school for ordinary kids.

She was sure it wouldn't have an awesome art studio like Lincoln School had, where she spent almost every day after school perfecting her drawings of trees and birds and pretty skies.

Or fantastic teachers like Ms. Webster, who always kept a jar of Hershey's Kisses on her desk, or Mr. Scott, who made the students laugh with his dumb jokes and those goofy ties he always wore.

To get there, Lizzy would have to walk six blocks up Third Avenue and turn left onto East Twenty-Fourth Street. If it was raining or freezing cold, the city bus was an option. It stopped on the corner.

Somewhere in the apartment, there was a School of Tomorrow welcome packet with a silly smiling globe on the envelope but thinking about those know-it-all kids staring at the new girl made Lizzy's stomach twist in knots.

Her mother tried to convince her that all the students were new because the school started in sixth grade, when most middle schools in New York began, but Lizzy wasn't buying it. She was positive she would make a fool of herself.

Subject : Hi!
From : elizamurphyzander@gmail.com
To : hannahbanana99@yahoo.com

Dear Hannah,

I told Amy I'm taking turns writing to you guys. I already wrote to her because I picked her name first from the bowl. Now it's your turn! You better write back! How are your braces? Does your mouth still hurt?

I'm now an official member of the New York Public Library! I have my very own card! I took out lots of books to read with my dad.

Right now, I'm sitting at the dining table by the door. It's super quiet. My mom and dad took Julian to the grocery store because we have no food in the fridge (except for frozen yogurt bars, which are in the freezer), and I decided to stay home. So here I am emailing you on my mom's laptop.

I was trying to work on a new drawing (my pencils are all over the place!), but I can't concentrate. I am eating one of those yogurt bars and pieces of chocolate are falling on the table. It's hard to eat and write at the same time!

OK, I'm back. Finished my yogurt (Yum!). I think I'll start typing in a different c o l o r. What about THIS? Or THIS? What about THIS ONE?

Hannah!!! I am scared to start my new school.

What if no one likes me? I know I'll get lost. And I will definitely forget the combination to my locker. And changing classes—ugh! What if I don't have enough time to go to the bathroom AND get to class!? Who am I going to sit with at lunch???? Probably at the loser table.

I wish my mom hadn't gotten her new job, and I wish my dad didn't have M.S.

I wish I could live with you and still go to Lincoln School. (Even though you guys are starting Edison Middle in the fall. OMG!)

I miss you so so so much!!!

Love 'til the ocean freezes,
Me
Xoxoxoxoxo

P.S. I still don't think it's fair we had to move here!

Chapter 4

Ms. Olsen blew her whistle. "Let's go, people. Get in your groups. We're going to keep practicing our dives. Just like last class."

Lizzy hurried to her spot behind the boy with the yellow swim trunks and light brown hair. He turned his head in her direction.

"This class sucks," he mouthed.

Lizzy nodded absentmindedly, while trying to tuck her uncooperative strands under a shiny pink swim cap. It wasn't fair that the girls had to wear caps, but the boys didn't. Wasn't that sexist?

She adjusted her straps and tugged the blue suit down so it didn't give her a wedgie. She hated wedgies.

"Miss Reed, please remind us what a successful dive looks like," requested Ms. Olsen. "And you too, Mr. Snyder. Both of you."

As the two groups of students looked on, the girl with the orange and purple suit dove smoothly into the shimmering pool, followed by a chubby boy wearing black-and-white checkered board shorts. His dive was also impressive, although it made a bigger splash. *What show-offs*, Lizzy thought.

"There's a strong diver inside each and every one of you," said Ms. Olsen. "Now let's do this. Give it your all!"

For the next twenty minutes, the students took turns catapulting into the water. Lizzy tried to copy what the girl and boy did, but, unfortunately, her dives were less than successful.

All flailing arms and legs, she felt about as graceful as an earthquake.

ξ

"You look a lot like my friend's sisters. But you don't go to Greystone School, do you? Because I know everyone who goes to Greystone," the girl who knew how to dive said.

"Maybe it's the red hair," she continued. "Ellie and Anna Sundersmith have red hair too. They're identical twins, but I can tell them apart. Ellie's teeth stick out more."

The girl had changed out of her wet bathing suit into dry clothes and had come over to the bench where Lizzy was sitting. Lizzy pulled her towel up to cover herself. She wasn't about to get undressed in front of this person she didn't know.

"Um, no, I just moved here."

"Oh, wow! A newbie. Well, you survived your second class with Ms. Olsen. That's an accomplishment! By the way, I'm Cassandra. My friends call me Cassie."

"Nice to meet you. I'm Lizzy. My real name is Eliza, but everyone calls me Lizzy," said Lizzy. "You're such a good diver. I'm the worst."

"You just need practice, that's all. I used to be as awkward as you but now look at me," said Cassandra, sitting down on the bench next to Lizzy.

Lizzy wasn't sure how to take that comment. She decided to change the subject. "I like your earrings."

"Thanks. You can borrow them if you want."

She squeezed one of the tiny gold hoops between her thumb and index finger. "I have like a million pairs."

"I don't have my ears pierced yet. I have to wait until I turn thirteen." She rubbed her bare lobes.

"Oh. That's too bad. How old are you now because you look at least thirteen!" Cassandra's eyes went up and down Lizzy's lanky body. It made her feel uncomfortable.

"Eleven and a half. My birthday's in November. I'm just tall. How old are you?"

"Turned twelve in May. So why did you move here anyway?" She tightened a rubber band on one of her braids.

"My mom got a new job," said Lizzy.

"Oh. What does she do? My mom's a lawyer."

"She is going to be the head of this animal organization called Best Friends." Lizzy picked the polish off her thumb while they talked.

"So, it's just you and your mother?"

"My mom and dad and my little brother, Julian. And my dog, Penny."

"Aw, I love dogs. My mother won't let me get one. She's so mean. What about your dad? What does he do?"

"Um, he works for a record company. He's really into music." She gave Cassandra a quick smile, then looked away.

"Oh, cool. Hey, where do you live?"

"On Eighteenth Street. My apartment is between Second and Third Avenues," said Lizzy, adjusting her towel. "I finally convinced my parents that I can walk around the corner by myself."

"No way!" Cassandra shrieked, jumping up, her brown eyes widening. "That's where I am, at 200 East Eighteenth!"

"I'm 202, the reddish building."

"Girl, we're next-door neighbors! My mom and I live in the big white building with the terraces and glass lobby on the corner. We're in the penthouse!"

"Wait, you live in a house?" Lizzy asked. She noticed that Cassandra couldn't seem to stand still. She was stomping her feet on the grimy floor of the locker room and wiggling her hips like crazy. Lizzy didn't know what was wrong with her.

"No *pent*-house," said Cassandra. "It's the apartment at the very top."

"Oh. Your building's super nice. I hate my apartment. I used to live in a big house with a porch and a backyard. There was even a swing set and a sandbox for Julian to play in. Um, are you okay?"

"Sorry, Lizzy, but I have to pee so bad. Meet me out front after you get changed," said Cassandra as she dashed into one of the pink bathroom stalls across from the lockers.

Lizzy was relieved to have a few moments to herself. She felt bad that she had lied about her dad, but she couldn't imagine telling Cassandra the truth. At least not now. She changed quickly and scrunched her hair so the waves came back to life after being trapped inside her swim cap.

Outside, they walked for a few minutes without talking. Lizzy pulled up the handle of her tote bag and navigated her way around two people on bicycles coming toward her. She was still getting used to all the crowds and the noise. She had never heard so many honking horns in her entire life.

"Want to join my secret club?" Cassandra asked as they crossed the street.

"What secret club?"

17

"Wait, I'll tell you when we get home. You're coming over, right?"

"Um, I guess I can for a little while, but I have to let my mom know so she doesn't freak out." Lizzy couldn't believe Cassandra, who was pretty and the star of swim class, had invited her. For real.

Chapter 5

When they arrived at Cassandra's building, a doorman opened the door. "Hi Malcolm!" Cassandra greeted him. "This is my friend Lizzy. She lives next door. She doesn't have a doorman."

Lizzy wasn't sure what that had to do with anything, but she shook Malcolm's hand anyway. He wore a gray and white uniform and shiny black shoes. "Hello, Lizzy. Any friend of Cassie's is a friend of mine."

"Nice to meet you," Lizzy answered awkwardly. As they walked through the sparkling lobby, which smelled like perfume, Lizzy tried to act normal. Inside, she felt excited and a little nervous.

The elevator stopped on the seventh floor to let out an old woman and her little white dog. When the doors opened on the top floor, they were already in Cassandra's apartment.

"I'm home!" Cassandra yelled out to no one in particular, throwing her swim stuff on the floor in the foyer. Lizzy followed, plopping her tote bag down next to Cassandra's.

She looked around. The apartment had super high ceilings, lots of windows, and colorful artwork—paintings, masks, sculptures—all over the walls and shelves.

And what she guessed to be hundreds of plants were growing everywhere. Some resembled the ones her mom had brought from their house—like the jade tree and the snake plants—but others she had never seen before. They looked like they belonged in a far-away garden.

They turned right and walked down a long hall to the enormous white kitchen. Cassandra pulled the refrigerator open. "Want a soda?" she asked, handing Lizzy a can of Diet Coke.

"Okay," Lizzy said.

Cassandra picked up a metal container and a stack of paper napkins.

"Let's go to my room!"

Cassandra's bed was the size of Lizzy's parents' bed with pillows of every size and color, even one shaped like an elephant. One wall was covered with animal-print wallpaper. Smack in the middle of the room sat two hot-pink bean-bag chairs on a shaggy white rug.

On the other side was a white desk with a green chair that went up and down and spun around, which Cassandra happily demonstrated. Her walk-in closet was almost as large as Lizzy's entire bedroom.

"Wow! I love your room!" exclaimed Lizzy.

They sank into the bean-bag chairs. Cassandra placed the container on the floor between them and lifted the lid. "Tada! Oreos!"

Lizzy's favorite. How did she know?

"So what school are you going to?" asked Cassandra, after stuffing a cookie into her mouth.

"School of Tomorrow."

"Never heard of it. Is it private?"

"I don't know. It's the school in District 2 I got assigned to. It's on Twenty-Fourth Street, I think."

"Oh, that's public. Greystone is on East Eighty-Ninth Street. It's private, plus it's only girls."

"No boys?"

"Nope. There are a few male teachers but for the most part, it's all girls all the time! My mother and aunt also went to Greystone. It's named for this woman named Millicent Jennings Greystone who started it more than 100 years ago before women could even vote. Can you even believe that?"

Lizzy smiled and nodded her head. Cassandra kept on talking.

"And I have to wear a uniform every day and take the school bus up First Avenue. It picks me at 7:25 in the morning!"

"I have no idea what my new school will be like," said Lizzy. "I hope it has good art teachers because I love to draw, but I can't think about school right now. It makes me way too nervous."

They ate their cookies in silence. Lizzy took a sip of her Diet Coke. She wasn't used to drinking soda. She didn't like how the bubbles tickled her tongue. She wondered if Cassandra would mention the Secret Club again.

"You must have a lot of friends at your school," said Lizzy.

"Well, I did," said Cassandra, her voice softening. "That is, until the Dylan Quinn disaster."

"Who's Dylan Quinn?" Lizzy was surprised by Cassandra's sudden mood shift. She wanted to know more.

"Only the meanest, most stuck-up girl I've ever met." Cassandra stared straight ahead, not meeting Lizzy's gaze. "She started at Greystone last year when her dad got transferred to New York from Los Angeles. He's some hot shot at an advertising agency."

"What happened with Dylan?"

21

"She stole my best friend!"

"Really? She did?" Lizzy leaned in closer.

"Yup, Hazel Leonard-Jones, my best friend since first grade, went over to the dark side. Her loss. It's whatever."

Lizzy couldn't imagine Amy or Hannah doing something like that, although there were mean girls at Lincoln School too, like Tiffany Thomas and Jilly Sinclair. She felt bad for Cassandra. She didn't know how to respond, so she just smiled in what she hoped was an understanding way.

After a moment, Cassandra's face softened again. "Have you ever kissed a boy?" she asked, interrupting the quiet.

"One time at this day camp I went to last summer, this boy Sebastian—he had sweaty hands and wore a backwards Yankees baseball cap all the time even though it looked so dumb," she continued. "Anyways, he tried to kiss me when we were finishing up our sandwiches in the park. But I pushed him away and ran back to my friends. That's another reason I like going to a girls school. Not that girls can't kiss girls, but you know what I mean."

"I'd rather eat eyeballs than kiss anyone," said Lizzy.

"Eat eyeballs?!" said Cassandra, raising her eyebrows.

"That's what I say when somebody asks me to do something I totally don't want to do," explained Lizzy, "like the time my mom made me invite this girl Margery over after school even though she always called me Casper the Friendly Ghost because my skin was so white."

"Well, you are kind of pale," said Cassandra. "I guess it goes with your red hair. My skin is 'in between' because my mother is black, and my father is white. Or *was* white. He died when I was a baby."

"Oh. I'm sorry. That must have been hard."

"Not really. I don't even remember him."

Lizzy couldn't imagine a world without her father. He was the best dad ever.

Lizzy liked the feeling of the soft bean bag chair. It reminded her of a giant hug. She thought about all those little plastic beads inside shifting under her weight. She liked being with Cassandra in her room.

Cassandra leaned her head back and closed her eyes. Lizzy looked at her. "What are you thinking about?" she asked.

"I'm not thinking. I'm feeling my feet on the ground. My tongue in my mouth. The air going in and out of my lungs," said Cassandra.

"My mom likes to meditate," she went on. "Do you know what that is? It's like when you sit in a quiet room and think about nothing for an entire hour. My mom says it helps her relax and not be anxious, but I thought it was boring with a capital B."

Suddenly, Lizzy jumped up with a start. Her mother! She'd forgotten to let her know where she was. *She's going to kill me,* she thought. And just like that her joyful feeling vanished into thin air.

"Uh... I should call my mom. Can I use your phone?" she asked, trying to sound casual.

"You don't have a phone?"

"No, not yet, do you?"

"Of course. Everyone does." Lizzy's parents promised her she could get a phone before school started. She needed one right now!

"The land line's over there," said Cassandra. "When you come back, I'll tell you all about the Secret Club." She gestured down the hall to the entryway.

As Lizzy dialed her home phone number, which she had finally memorized after writing it on her hand for a few days, her heart thumped crazily in her chest.

"Hello? Lizzy, is that you?" Her mother answered after half a ring.

"Hi Mom. Sorry, I forgot to call you."

"Eliza Murphy Zander, where are you?! I have been sick with worry. I knew it was a mistake to let you walk home by yourself."

"I'm next door, at Cassandra's, my friend from swimming. She invited me over after class." As she spoke to her mom, she heard voices in the kitchen, one was Cassandra's, the other was a woman. Lizzy guessed it was her mother.

"You need to come home. Now."

She hung up the phone. The voices in the kitchen sounded angry. They were having an argument. Was Cassandra in trouble too?

"You have had all morning to finish your work," Lizzy heard the woman say. "What have you been doing?"

"Hanging out with Lizzy."

"Who?"

"Lizzy, from swim class."

"I don't have time for this, Cassandra. I'm taking a bath. You better change your attitude by the time I'm out."

Frantically, Lizzy pushed the button for the elevator, hoping it would arrive before Cassandra noticed she was gone. She didn't want her to know she had heard them fighting. The elevator slid open and Lizzy stepped inside.

The Secret Club would have to wait.

Chapter 6

"Mom, I have no idea where my blue dress is. I don't know where anything is!"

"I offered to help you organize your closet several times. You said you wanted to do it yourself," her mother responded in an angry voice. "Now all your clothes are piled everywhere, and your dress is nowhere to be found."

"Because I don't have a closet!" Lizzy shouted. "Remember, Mom?! I gave that up, along with everything I loved, when you made us move into this stupid apartment! And I don't want to go George and Audra's party anyway."

George and Audra were her mom's friends from college who lived nearby. It was definitely going to be a super boring grown-up party, all the more reason to stay home!

"You have a closet right here, it just doesn't happen to be in your bedroom," said her mom, nodding toward the small hall closet her parents had designated for her stuff. "I wish you'd listen to me once in a while and stop being so dramatic. And watch your tone of voice with me, young lady. I'm your mother!" She walked away from Lizzy and back into the kitchen, sighing loudly.

Stung, Lizzy lay down on her bed. She could feel tears beginning in the corners of her eyes. Right on cue, Penny trotted into the room to see what all the fuss was about. She hopped up, curled against Lizzy's back, and burrowed her small body into the jumble of pillows and blankets. At least her dog understood her.

After a few minutes they both were asleep.

By the time Lizzy woke up, it was pouring outside. And she had forgotten all about her missing dress.

"Hey Murphy, how's my girl?" She turned her head to the sound of her dad's voice in her room. He often called by her middle name, which made her feel special.

"Hi Daddy. What time is it?" She rolled toward him, waking Penny, who hopped down and headed into the kitchen.

When Lizzy's dad looked at her, all her troubles melted away. "It's after five. Time for someone to set the table." Lizzy put her bare feet on the floor. "Hold on, I want to talk to you for a minute."

"I already know what you're going to say," Lizzy interrupted. "That I should be nicer to Mom."

"Well, yes, Mom told me you got a little mad at her. But she understands how you feel. We both do. We know how hard this move has been for you." His voice was kind.

"You do?"

"Of course we do. We feel terrible that we uprooted you from your friends and your life in Mount Olive and brought you to New York. I loved our old house too. I'll never forget all the memories we made there."

Lizzy smiled shyly at her dad, even though she felt sad inside. She could hear clattering noises coming from the kitchen and smelled garlic sautéing on the stove.

"Remember, Mom and Aunt Fiona grew up in that house. It was a huge part of their lives, too. We all had to say goodbye to something we loved," he said.

Lizzy didn't know what to say. She stared at the blankets on her bed, she stared at her hands with the chipped blue nail polish, she looked around the room, at the photograph of her friends that she put on the dresser, at the brick wall outside her window. She didn't look at her father.

"Being your dad is the best job in the world. I would do anything to protect you from getting hurt or feeling afraid."

Her father was sitting on the edge of her bed. He was wearing tan shorts and a black Beatles shirt that was fraying at the collar, one of many music-related T-shirts that he had acquired over the years. Lizzy loved that about him. He didn't wear boring suits like some of her friends' fathers. He was a cool dad.

"Daddy?" she asked. "What if I don't like my new school?"

Lizzy's father looked into her eyes and touched her cheek. Her parents always told her what a fat baby she had been. She weighed almost ten pounds at birth.

But she wasn't a baby or even a little kid anymore. She was growing up fast. In a few months she would be twelve years old.

How in the world would she find her place in New York City? So many thoughts swirled inside her head. She wished she could push pause and start all over again.

"You *will* like your new school. It may take some patience and a little courage, but I know you will," answered her dad in his matter-of-fact way. "And there are so many new friends waiting to meet you. Now, come on, let's get the table set so we can enjoy Mom's delicious pasta!"

Lizzy watched him walk into the kitchen, his left foot dragging a little along the floor, and open up the silverware drawer. She stood up, slid into her slippers, and went to help.

"I'm sorry, Lizzy. I shouldn't have yelled at you like that," said her mom, as she poured tomato sauce over the spaghetti and passed out the plates. "Thanks for setting the table."

27

"I don't want the red stuff, Mommy. It's yucky!" said Julian.

"You need to try a little, Jules," said their dad, who was sitting next to Lizzy's brother. "Here, just a tiny bit."

He scooped up a spoon of sauce from the pot in the middle of the table and drizzled it on Julian's pasta, which was in a green plastic bowl.

"It's okay," said Lizzy quietly, looking down as she twirled the strands of spaghetti around her fork. She still felt upset that she and her mother had argued.

The family ate quietly. Lizzy's parents sipped their glasses of red wine. Her mom put another scoop of pasta on her dad's plate. He spooned parmesan cheese on top.

Margot glanced over at Lizzy, then at Julian. "What do you think, Cal? Do these munchkins deserve some ice cream?" Lizzy looked up, her face brightening.

"Interesting idea," said their dad. "Let me give that some thought."

"Please, Daddy! I'm eating my red stuff. See?" Julian stuffed a forkful into his mouth. A bit of sauce dripped down his chin. He wiped it off with the back of his chubby hand. Lizzy didn't say anything.

"I'm sure Lizzy wants ice cream too, when she finishes her dinner. Right, sweetheart?" asked her mom. "I'll just need your help clearing the table. We can do the rest later."

"Thanks, Mom," said Lizzy. This time she smiled.

A little later, Lizzy and her family walked to Frosty's. The temperature had gone down, and the evening air was just right.

Her dad pushed Julian's stroller, which helped steady him. Her mom held tight to Lizzy's hand and to Penny's leash.

Even though she couldn't say it out loud, sometimes Lizzy liked holding her mom's hand. It made her feel safe. As they waited for the traffic light to change, she reached down to scratch under Penny's chin.

"Are you my good puppy dog?" she asked. She wondered if Penny missed New Jersey as much she did.

Subject : Guess Who ?!
From : elizamurphyzander@gmail.com
To : amyyvonnekim@gmail.com

Dear Amy,

This is my 8th day on 18th Street! My room is STILL a mess. And the city is STILL dirty.

The rest of the apartment is looking better, I guess. I had a fight with my mom before because my blue dress (remember the one with the white collar I got last year?) seems to have disappeared and she wants me to wear it to this dumb party next week her friend George invited us to.

I'm wondering:

1. Why do I have to go?
2. If I absolutely have to go, why can't I wear shorts? It's boiling hot!

Aunt Fiona will be coming soon to help out when my mom starts her new job. I can't wait. I love her so so much! But I don't know where she is going to sleep. Maybe in Julian's room but it's even smaller than mine! Not in my room - I need my privacy!!!

My mom had a talk with me and told me I had to be a "mature" (that was before our fight). She is "counting on me." Newsflash: She shouldn't count on me! I don't know anything. I cried myself to sleep last night. I tried to be quiet so my parents wouldn't hear me.

29

Things I Miss: You and Hannah!! OF COURSE!! My house. The orange tiger lilies in our old backyard (they were so fun to draw!) Riding our bikes everywhere. The secret hiding place in the way back of my bedroom closet. Playing Connect 4 on the porch. And Miss Mary Mack! Swinging in your hammock. Milkshakes!

Super great summers. My Old Life!!!!

Gotta help give Julian a bath. Then I'm going to take a shower and put cream on my gross dry skin. Email me back soon!!!!

Love 'til the ocean freezes,
Me
Xoxoxoxoxoxoxoxo

Chapter 7

June was over and soon it would be the Fourth of July. Lizzy had finally emptied the boxes and bags from the floor of her room and folded her clothes in neat piles in her dresser and put her shoes and books and art supplies in the drawers underneath her bed.

When she looked in the mirror on her dresser, she was annoyed (but not surprised) that her freckles had multiplied like mad, covering practically every inch of her face from her chin to her forehead. Her arms swarmed with dark brown dots. Her hair had lightened in the sun.

Lizzy pulled on her jean shorts and a white polo shirt and slid into her flip-flops. After tying the front of her hair back with a Scrunchie, she rubbed extra-strength sunscreen all over her face and put on her bubblegum Lip Smackers before storing the tube in her front pocket. She stuffed a hardback in her tote bag, along with her water bottle.

"Can I go to the library?" Lizzy asked. "I need a new book." Even though she was grounded, Lizzy's mom would make an exception for a new book, wouldn't she? She was scared to ask.

It was a Saturday morning after breakfast, and her mom and dad were reading the paper and discussing the news, as they had every weekend morning for as long as Lizzy could remember.

Nearby, Julian played with his horses, his current obsession.

"Giddy-up! Giddy-up!" he shouted over and over again as his toy chestnut and palomino ponies galloped around the rug.

The round table was covered with sections of the newspaper, half-full coffee cups, and dirty plates. Her dad's cane rested against the wall. He must have felt wobbly this morning.

Penny, always on the lookout for food, sat at attention at her mom's feet. She knew she or Julian would be the ones most likely to give her a treat. Sometimes it drove Lizzy crazy how spoiled the dog was, even though she was as guilty as the rest of her family.

Her mom glanced up from her article. "You're grounded, Lizzy, remember?"

"Not even for the library?" Lizzy pleaded.

"I said no. No arguing." Lizzy crossed her arms and sighed loudly.

Julian padded over to the table and handed Penny a corner of cold toast from his dad's plate, which the dog scarfed down in two seconds flat. He went back to his horses.

"Mom, please, I said I was sorry. I've been stuck inside forever!" She really wanted to find another book to read with her dad, and now her mother was ruining everything. And her dad wasn't helping.

"Next time, you'll remember to call me when you're going to be late. We may be in a new place, but the old rules still apply. Now sit down and have some breakfast."

"I'm not hungry."

"Please sit," said Lizzy's mom. Reluctantly, Lizzy pulled out a chair and plopped down, a look of disappointment on her face. Her mother spooned a helping of scrambled eggs onto a plate and pushed it toward her. Lizzy stared at the food. Her mind raced.

"If I had a phone, like every single person my age has, I could call you or text you all the time. Just saying!" she shouted, her voice rising with each word.

"What makes you think you are the only one without a cell phone?" asked Lizzy's dad. "I find that hard to believe."

"Because it's true. Cassandra has one and so does like the whole world! I'm not a baby!"

"You're being a little dramatic, wouldn't you say?" said Lizzy's mother. "The plan is to wait until school starts. Phone or no phone, you're still grounded."

"It's not fair! Don't you want to know where I am all the time? Something bad could happen and you wouldn't even know!"

"Lizzy, play with me!" Julian was standing over his sister, thrusting his horses at her. "You can be the brown one. He likes to gallop like this." He moved his hand up and down in the air to show her.

"Not now, Julian!" Lizzy snapped. Hurt, Julian turned away and went to sit with Penny on the couch.

"Okay, Murphy, we get it. We'll talk about the phone another time. Right now, I need you to calm down and listen to your mother," said her dad. *Why couldn't he be on her side?* she thought. Her head felt like it might explode.

"I hate both of you!" she screamed, storming off to her bedroom and slamming the door so hard the entire apartment shook.

Chapter 8

Following two miserable days of being grounded, Lizzy was excited to see Cassandra again. After her mom dropped her off at the Y (she had lost her walking-alone privileges, which she hoped would be restored very soon), Lizzy waited for her on their usual bench in the locker room for what felt like ages.

Finally, just as class was about to start, Cassandra showed up, out of breath.

"There you are! We're going to be late!" Here, put your stuff in." Lizzy gestured to an open locker where her bag already was.

"Sorry. The Secret Club meeting just ended. There was so much to talk about, we totally lost track of time! I ran all the way over here."

"Oh," was all Lizzy could manage to say.

Why hadn't she been invited to the meeting? She wanted to know what this Secret Club was all about, but not now. They were late for their lesson. The girls rushed out to the pool to join their groups.

Lizzy's group was supposed to be practicing the crawl, but she couldn't concentrate.

"Miss Zander, don't forget to breathe!" shouted Ms. Olsen. "And kick those legs nice and hard. That will make you go faster. Come on, let's see some effort."

Lizzy practiced turning her head to take a breath while coordinating the movement of her arms, but her heart wasn't in it. She kept wondering about the

Secret Club and Cassandra. She couldn't see Cassie from her spot in the pool, but she was sure whatever she was doing, it was flawless.

Next to Lizzy, a girl was having trouble. She kept veering off into the next lane, bumping into the boy with the yellow swim trunks and the funny-looking goggles. Suddenly, Ms. Olsen blew her whistle, interrupting her thoughts.

"Five more minutes, people," said Ms. Olsen. "Make them count!" With her last ounce of energy, Lizzy finished her lap. When she reached the wall on the other side, she pulled off her cap and submerged herself under the cold water.

ξ

After class, Lizzy met her mom in front, as they had agreed. Her aunt's flight was scheduled to arrive at Newark Airport in a few hours, and her mom was taking a cab there to pick her up.

She said goodbye to Cassandra, and they headed off in different directions.

"I'll call you later," Lizzy assured her. They had exchanged numbers earlier.

Although still morning, the July day was already approaching ninety degrees. The smothering humidity made Lizzy's hair frizz and her underarms sweat.

Her dad and brother were lucky—they got to stay home in the air-conditioned apartment. The summer heat made her dad's M.S. symptoms worse, so he tried his best to stay inside when it was really hot.

Lizzy wished she could watch cartoons and eat peanut-butter-and-jelly sandwiches with them, or even better, spend all afternoon drawing, but she had to help her mom.

Aunt Fiona was Lizzy's mom's younger sister. She lived in Montana and taught yoga. They were two years apart but looked like twins, except Fiona had glasses and wore her long red hair in a braid down her back. When she was teaching, it was in a bun on top of her head.

Lizzy's aunt wasn't married and didn't have any kids of her own, so she spoiled her favorite and only niece and nephew.

She made Julian and Lizzy's Halloween costumes every year without fail, until last fall, when Lizzy announced that she was too old to go trick-or-treating. Their aunt was a very creative person—she had studied art in college. Lizzy liked to think she inherited her talent from her.

"Let's get a cart," Lizzy's mom said. As Lizzy wheeled the shopping cart through the aisles of Food Emporium, she checked items off a list: chicken breast, tuna fish, grated mozzarella, broccoli, oranges, avocadoes, bananas, cereal, rice.

"Can we get Pringles?" she asked her mom. "Please?"

"Just this once, because it's a special occasion. What else is on the list?"

"Paper towels and toilet paper," Lizzy read. "And that's it." She crumpled the paper in her hand.

"Let's go to aisle five," her mom said. "Then we're done."

They walked back to the apartment carrying the groceries in paper bags. "Lizzy, I understand how you feel about wanting a phone."

Lizzy looked over at her mother. "You do?"

"Yes, although I'm not happy with the way you behaved the other day. Temper tantrums aren't going to get you anywhere, I can promise you that much."

The light turned green, and they crossed the street. The sun beat down on the black pavement, heating up the air even more. Several new buildings were being constructed in the neighborhood, and there was scaffolding everywhere.

"I'm sorry, Mom. I didn't mean what I said. Really."

"What floor?" a man with a beard asked as they stepped into the elevator.

"Four," said her mom. The man pushed the button. "Thanks," she said. The door shut and Lizzy closed her eyes until the elevator opened on their floor.

When they got back to the apartment, her dad walked into the kitchen to help unpack the bags.

"Mission accomplished?" he asked, yawning.

"Yup," said Lizzy. "We got bananas for your smelly smoothies." Her dad's hair was standing straight up. Lizzy guessed he had been napping again. He slept all the time. At least it felt that way.

"And lots of food for Fiona's visit," added Lizzy's mom.

"I bet Aunt Fiona has a phone!"

"Will you stop with the phone. You sound like a broken record," said Lizzy's dad. Maybe if she annoyed them enough, they'd give in and let her get one. Her plan didn't seem to be working...yet.

Chapter 9

"Lizzy, can you pull down your extra quilt and pillow from the top of the linen closet? You'll have to climb up on the step stool, so please be careful."

The shopping complete and lunch eaten, her mom was rushing to get the apartment organized before she left to pick up Aunt Fiona at the airport. She wanted everything to be perfect.

Sitting in a chair at the sink, Lizzy's dad carefully washed the pots and pans with soapy water. Julian had fallen asleep on the couch, next to Penny. "I could use help drying, Murphy," he called out.

"Just a second, Dad, I'm helping Mom. Jeez! I'm only one person." *Why were parents so irritating?* she thought.

After she got the bedding down, she grabbed a dish towel from the counter and began drying the pots as her dad washed them. Then she went back to helping her mom.

Lizzy was tired of doing chores but so excited to see her aunt. With her mom starting her new job and Julian transitioning to the day-care center near her mother's office, an extra set of hands would be a huge help. Lizzy was glad they were her aunt's hands!

As Lizzy hoped, Fiona would stay in Julian's room. Although small like hers, her brother's room had a brand-new twin bed that Julian hadn't started sleeping in yet. Since the move, he preferred his parents' queen-size bed, even though he had a playpen that they kept folded up in the corner. Penny also usually bunked with them, making for especially cozy sleeping arrangements.

Lizzy brought an armload of Julian's stuffed animals—the ones he wasn't currently playing with (and not Bob the Bunny!)—into her room and threw them on her bed. Aunt Fiona didn't need to worry about tripping over them if she got up to use the bathroom in the middle of the night. Then Lizzy and her mom finished making up the bed, smoothing the quilt, and arranging the pillows.

After her mother left for the airport, Lizzy opened her mom's laptop and logged into her email account. Why weren't there any new messages for her? She decided to write another letter to Hannah.

Subject : Remember me?!
From : elizamurphyzander@gmail.com
To : hannahbanana99@yahoo.com

Dear Hannah,

Don't be mad but guess what? I think I made a new friend. Not a friend like you or Amy of course but she's nice and pretty and talks A LOT. Oh, her name is Cassandra Reed.

We met at the Y where I take swim lessons (I'm SO bad, like the worst in the whole class. You would fall over laughing if you watched me try to dive.)

You wouldn't believe how beautiful her apartment is. It's like a palace. Her room is like twice as big as my old bedroom. For real! I think her family must have a lot of money.

And she goes to an all-girls school! And she has her own phone!!! When will your mom let you get one? My parents better let me have one! It's the least they can do after making me move here!!!

So Cassie (she told me I could call her that) asked me to join her "Secret Club." I had to leave before she told me more because my mom was mad at me. Stay tuned!

My mom is on her way to pick up Aunt Fiona at the airport right now. I can't wait!!!

I hope you and Amy are having a fun summer doing the fun things we used to do together.

Have you walked by my old house? It seems like a long time ago. I guess time is different in New York. Who knows?

Well, I'm about to take Penny out for a walk (poop = yuck!). So bye for now from your NYC friend, Lizzy!

Love 'til the ocean freezes,
Me
Xoxoxo

P.S. Happy Almost 4th of July! Are you going to watch the fireworks at Mindowaskin Park?

ξ

The phone rang. "Zander residence?" Lizzy's dad answered.

They had finished dinner, and the adults were sitting around the table talking and drinking wine. As he did nearly every evening, Lizzy's dad put a record on the turntable, and a slow song filled the room.

Lizzy liked the sound of the singer's voice, but she couldn't figure out the exact words he was singing. She made a mental note to ask her dad, the music expert.

Julian had squirmed out of his booster seat and was searching for one of his horses under the coffee table. Soon it would be time for his bath. Aunt Fiona was telling Lizzy about the yoga retreat she was going to in Brooklyn the next day.

"Just a minute, please." Her dad handed the phone to Lizzy.

40

"Hello?" answered Lizzy, a puzzled look on her face. Her mother laughed at something her sister said. Lizzy noticed her mom relaxed more around her sister.

"You broke your promise."

"Um, wait, who is this?"

"Your friend from the pool!"

"Oh, Cassie! Oh gosh, things have been crazy around here! My aunt got here a while ago, and we've been eating and catching up. I totally forgot to call you."

"Found it!" shouted Julian, pulling his arm back from under the couch. "Come on, Midnight, let's go eat some carrots," he said to his black plastic horse. "Yum yum."

"Julian, shush. I'm on the phone," said Lizzy. "Sorry, Cassie. What were you saying?"

"I'm calling to let you know that the next meeting of the Secret Club is tomorrow at noon at my place. All the members are expected to attend, and that includes new members like you. So I'll see you tomorrow. Don't be late, and don't forget to bring a secret."

"Uh...what do you mean, bring a secret?"

"Something you haven't told anyone, ever. We share our secrets with each other, that's why it's called the Secret Club. Get it? Bye for now!" The phone clicked off and Cassandra was gone.

Lizzy didn't get it. Secrets wouldn't be secrets anymore if she told them to other people, right? Lizzy thought Cassandra was weird and exasperating. But weird and exasperating in an interesting, I-want-to-know-more way.

What were Lizzy's secrets anyway? And why on earth would she ever want to share something private with a bunch of strangers? Wouldn't that be like giving away a part of herself?

41

That night, Lizzy couldn't sleep. She lay awake under her blankets listening to the hum of the air conditioner and Penny's rhythmic snoring. Seeking more space, the dog had abandoned her parents' bed and jumped up to snuggle next to Lizzy, promptly drifting off. Lizzy reached over to stroke Penny's ears.

Yet, sleep did not come. So Lizzy sat up, switched on her light, and started a new drawing. She began sketching a yellow house against a cloudy blue sky, moving each pointy pencil in gentle strokes across her paper.

Her mind drifted. She thought about her new home, her new friend, the Secret Club, and where she belonged.

Chapter 10

Cassandra's common room looked different. The coffee table had been pushed to one side, and the chairs were now in a semi-circle in the middle.

Lizzy noticed a pitcher of lemonade and a stack of paper cups printed with daisies on the counter by the sink. There was also a bowl of popcorn and a plate of chocolate-chip cookies that looked homemade.

She wished she could drink ten cups of lemonade right now. Her mouth was so dry. But then she'd have to go to the bathroom and that would be even worse.

Lizzy stood alone, feeling stupid, while four other kids—three girls and one boy—talked and laughed and paid not one ounce of attention to her. Even though their silent treatment lasted for maybe two minutes, those two minutes felt like an eternity.

She folded her freckled arms across her chest, checked her Swatch watch, unfolded her arms, re-checked her Swatch watch, stared at her feet, examined her newly painted nails ("Cotton Candy Pink") tucked her hair behind her ears, counted her breaths.

How did she ever think she belonged here with these city kids who had nothing to worry about except their perfect hair, their perfect clothes, and their perfect lives? She felt like throwing up.

Finally, she saw Cassandra talking to two kids.

"Hi Lizzy, I'm so glad you made it!"

The next thing she knew, Cassandra's arms were enveloping her in a giant hug. Now the others noticed her.

She felt their curious eyes but tried to focus on the C-shaped pendants dangling from Cassandra's ears. Inhaling, she thought her friend smelled a little like the lavender soap Aunt Fiona put in the bathroom yesterday.

"Yup, here I am." Lizzy smiled hesitantly.

"I like to start right on time, so you'll meet everyone in just a minute. Why don't you make yourself comfy?"

Lizzy slid into a sand-colored armchair and folded her hands nervously in her lap. She looked at her colorful friendship bracelets, one on each wrist. She wished Amy and Hannah could see her now. Would they be proud of her or horrified?

As the others settled into their seats, Lizzy felt in her back pocket for the piece of paper she had ripped from her sketchbook. Her notes from last night. If she had to share a secret, she could at least read from the paper and avoid making eye contact with anyone. That was her plan.

She glanced around the room. Sitting next to her was a girl with tortoise-framed glasses and barrettes in her curly hair. On the other side was the boy. He was tall and skinny with a Band-Aid on one of his knees. He wore an orange-and-blue Knicks basketball shirt and white Converse high-tops that looked brand new.

Where did these kids came from? Did they live nearby?

"Hi. I'm Walt," he said, looking toward her.

Lizzy opened her mouth to answer, but before she could say a single word, Cassandra's voice filled the room.

"Attention, everyone! It is Sunday, July 9, at 12:06 p.m. and the third meeting of the Secret Club is called to order!" she declared, waving her arms in the air dramatically. "Please silence your electronic devices!"

Wow, Lizzy thought, Cassandra really took this Secret Club stuff seriously. A few kids pulled their phones out of their pockets and double-checked that they were shut off.

Was Lizzy the only one who didn't have a phone? She noticed Walt didn't seem to have one either. Maybe his parents treated him like a baby too.

"The first order of business is attendance. When I call your name, please respond in the affirmative. Okay, here we go." She began reading from an official-looking clipboard, checking off each name one by one with a Snoopy pen.

"Amanda Landers?"

"Here!"

"Chloe Brooks?"

"Over here!"

"Josephine Shin?"

"Yes!"

"Walt Johnson?"

"Right here! Right now! Bright-eyed and bushy-tailed!"

Lizzy had no idea what that meant, but she couldn't help smiling at Walt, who was goofy and also kind of cute.

"Lizzy Zander?"

"Here," she said, her voice barely louder than a whisper.

Two members shared their secrets. First, the girl with the barrettes, whose name was Josephine, confided that she still had a library book from third grade on her shelf at home.

It was a hardcover about Antarctica with glossy black-and-white photographs. Josephine had turned the book around so the spine, with the library sticker, was facing inwards, so her mother wouldn't notice it. "If my mother found out I hadn't returned a book for three years, she would definitely murder me."

Next, in a voice that sounded like a mouse, Amanda revealed that one day after school she stole a tube of lipstick from Macy's department store when her younger cousin Sheryl dared her. "Cool as a cucumber, I dropped the tube in my backpack and walked straight out of the store," Amanda said. "After that, Sheryl worshipped the ground I walked on."

Lizzy wondered what happened when all the Secret Club's secrets ran out. Did they share their dreams instead? And what about Cassandra? Did she start the Secret Club because she had some really big secrets of her own?

For a few blissful seconds, Lizzy forgot all about being terrified. That is, until she heard Cassandra's voice again.

"Now, it's time to meet our newest Secret Clubber!"

Panic gripped Lizzy's body. Her breathing quickened. Her heart ran a marathon inside her chest. Ribbons of sweat trickled down the inside of her shirt. Her sunburned legs froze to the chair.

"Lizzy Zander!" Cassandra sang out. To her surprise, everyone clapped, even Walt. "Lizzy just moved here from New Jersey, and we're so happy she did. Lizzy, can you stand up?" Cassandra gestured with her outstretched hands, a huge smile plastered to her face.

Lizzy tried to imagine that all the kids were wearing just their underwear, a trick her dad had taught her when she got so nervous before her performance as Munchkin #3 in Lincoln School's production of *The Wizard of Oz* that she almost passed out backstage. She had to put her head between her legs and take slow, deep breaths before she was able to go on.

The next night she pictured the entire audience and Mr. Lee, the dorky director, in their underwear, and she felt a lot calmer.

Unfortunately, this trick wasn't working so well right now. As hard as she tried, all Lizzy saw were four girls and one boy in their regular summer clothes staring at her like she had enormous horns growing out of her ears.

Moving in slow motion, she mustered the courage to rise to her feet. She felt her face turning bright red. "Hi. I'm Lizzy," she said quietly. Then she gave a quick little wave, which she immediately decided was totally lame.

"Welcome to our club!" said Cassandra. "Are you ready to share your secret?"

From her back pocket, Lizzy pulled out the piece of paper, unfolded it, and held it in front of her. The room was completely silent. "Um, I wrote it down so I wouldn't forget what to say." Then, reading from her page, she began, "When I was eight years old, my mother had a baby boy. My brother Julian."

She paused to take a breath. "One day I asked my mom if she could take me to the playground. She said no, we couldn't go because she needed to put the baby down for a nap. This made me mad because she never had time for me since he was born. So, when my mom went into the bathroom for a second and left me alone with Julian in his crib, I slipped a red crayon into his diaper. I don't know what happened the next time the baby needed changing. I'm sure my mom wondered where the crayon had come from, but I kept my secret and never told a single soul. Until today."

After she finished talking, Lizzy felt a tremendous wave of relief. She looked up from her paper to see the kids smiling at her. "Wow! What a fantastic secret, Lizzy! You had us on the edge of our seats!" Cassandra exclaimed. Then everyone clapped. Lizzy smiled back and sat down in her chair.

While the Secret Clubbers were munching on the snacks and Lizzy wasn't feeling quite so alone anymore, Cassandra's mother tip-toed into the room and walked over to Lizzy as she was about to bite into a cookie.

"Lizzy, honey, your mom just called." Her voice was soft. "You're needed at home."

Chapter 11

Before she even opened the door to her apartment, Lizzy heard screaming loud enough to wake the dead. Terrified, she rushed inside to discover her mom sitting on a chair in the dining room holding a squirming and shrieking Julian on her lap. He was still in his superhero pajamas.

"Jules, look baby, Lizzy's here," said their mom, motioning for Lizzy to approach.

Their dad squeezed Julian's arm. "Big sisters always have the magic touch," he said reassuringly. "Sorry Mom had to call you from your friend's house," her dad whispered into Lizzy's ear. "He only wanted you." She nodded.

Lizzy would do anything for her brother, but she was mad her parents had interrupted her. She wanted to stay at the Secret Club.

The white washcloth their mom pressed to Julian's temple was soaked in bright red blood. Lizzy's dad leaned in close, doing his best to calm him down. Penny nervously circled the room, ears on high alert.

"What happened?" Lizzy asked, pulling up another chair and reaching for Julian. "Come here baby, let me see."

"He realized the hard way that he can't fly," said their dad. "Landed on the bookshelf next to his bed."

With a little more coaxing, Julian repositioned himself onto Lizzy's lap, burying his face in her T-shirt. Lizzy's mom handed her the washcloth.

"Turn this way, Jules," said Lizzy.

"It hurts!" he yelled. "My head hurts. It feels yucky!" He tried to touch the wet spot on his temple. Lizzy gently took his hand and held it.

"Keep putting pressure on it," said their mom. "I'll get you a fresh one."

She stood up and walked into to the bathroom. Lizzy took a quick peek at the wound above Julian's left eyebrow.

"Holy moly, I can't believe how much blood is coming out of such a small cut," Lizzy observed.

"Heads bleed a lot," said her dad.

"Duh, Dad," said Lizzy, rolling her eyes.

"Jules, it's going to be okay, I promise." She carefully pressed the new cloth onto the cut to stop the bleeding. "Hey, where's Aunt Fiona?" she asked.

"She's at that all-day yoga retreat, remember?"

"Oh yeah, right," said Lizzy. Her parents stepped into the living room. Lizzy could hear them talking quietly. A moment later, they were back.

"Daddy and I think we should have a doctor look at your boo-boo," said their mom. Julian sniffed and looked up at Lizzy with the saddest face she had ever seen. It didn't help that he had a bloody washcloth covering half his forehead.

"I'll be with you the whole time," said Lizzy. "And where's Bob the Bunny? He has to come too!"

"Over there," Julian whispered, pointing to his stroller, where the rabbit rested, its pink ears hanging down over the edge of the well-worn seat.

Their mom changed Julian's diaper, and they got ready to go to the hospital. Their dad decided to stay home and clean up the mess from Julian's accident.

Lizzy was forced to carry Julian because he wouldn't let go of her. His arms encircled her neck and his legs were wrapped around her hips. He was so heavy.

Their mom stuffed Bob the Bunny into her purse and, just in case, some peanut-butter granola bars. She pulled his folded-up stroller behind her.

A cab stopped on the corner. By then Julian had mostly stopped crying, but his head was still bleeding. And he had the hiccups.

Fortunately, the pediatric unit was not crowded. They were whisked into an exam room right away.

"Want to play 'I Spy'?" Lizzy suggested. She placed Julian down on the shiny metal table.

"I spy a balloon," she said. Julian looked around, still hiccupping.

"Where?" he asked, lifting his head.

Lizzy pulled a latex glove from a box on the counter, brought it up to her mouth, and blew. The glove filled up with air. Lizzy wrapped the end around her index finger and made a knot.

"Right here," she said, batting her balloon to Julian, who let a little laugh escape from his mouth.

"Lizzy, you're a star!" said her mom gratefully.

Just then, the curtain slid back. In walked a woman with kinky black hair, dark skin, and round glasses. She wore scrubs with Mickey Mouse all over them and red high-tops. A stethoscope dangled from her neck.

"Hi everyone, I'm Dr. Washington," she said, pulling on a pair of gloves from the box. Lizzy couldn't believe she was a real doctor, dressed like that, but she was!

After Lizzy's mom explained what happened—Julian was jumping on his bed even though he wasn't supposed to when he lost his balance, smacking his head on the edge of his bookshelf—Dr. Washington looked at Julian and frowned.

"Mr. Julian, listen to me," said the doctor. Julian stared at her, his blue eyes as big as saucers. "Beds are for sleeping. Beds are not for jumping. Got it?" He nodded. "We're going to fix you up and you'll be good as new in no time."

Seven stitches, a cherry Blow Pop, and a handful of unicorn stickers later (which Julian stuck all over the front of his pajamas), they were on their way back home. Julian had been surprisingly brave during the entire procedure. Dr. Washington even put a Band-Aid on Bob the Bunny's ear.

By the time the cab pulled up in front of their building, Julian was asleep. Lizzy helped her mom open the stroller and she placed him inside.

"What should we have for dinner?" Lizzy mom asked, after tucking Julian into bed, dirty hair and all. "I'm too tired to cook."

"My vote is for pizza," Lizzy said.

"I second that," Lizzy's dad said.

As they were eating their slices, and her parents were sipping red wine, Aunt Fiona returned, wearing purple striped leggings, her yoga matt poking out of the top of her backpack.

"Did I miss anything exciting?" she asked as she dropped her stuff on the floor by the door and joined them at the table.

Lizzy looked at her parents and cracked up.

"While you were doing your downward dogs, your nephew had a little accident," said Lizzy's mom.

"I guess it's not serious if you're laughing," said her aunt.

"Well, things were a little nutty around here after Julian cut his head," said Lizzy's mom.

She pulled a piece of pepperoni off her slice of pizza and put it in her mouth. "But thanks to Lizzy, we calmed him down and got him to the hospital. He's sleeping now. We're all pretty exhausted."

"Wow, I really did miss a lot! Sorry, I feel bad I wasn't here to help out."

"How could you have known?" said Lizzy's dad. "He's fine now, so stop worrying. Have some pizza, Fiona." He slid the box over. Fiona grabbed the last slice. Lizzy returned to the table with a glass of water for her aunt.

"Hey Murphy," said her dad casually. "Do you want to come to the Verizon store with me tomorrow?"

"For what?" she asked, even though she had an idea.

"Mom and I talked about it and decided you can get a phone." Lizzy looked at her parents. They were both kind of smiling but in a serious way. Aunt Fiona was smiling too.

"Really, Daddy? Oh my god!" Her eyes practically popped out of her head.

"We'll go around 5:00 when it's not so hot, so make sure you're ready. But there are going to be rules that must be followed. It's not a toy."

"Duh, Dad. I know that."

"Did you just say 'Duh' to me?" Lizzy felt her face get hot. It was probably super red.

"Um, sorry, I meant to say, Thanks, Daddy! You're the best." She wrapped her arms around his shoulders and squeezed him tight.

"You should thank your mother. She's the one who convinced me you need a phone because it's been a tough time for you, with the move and all. I wasn't so sure it was necessary. I certainly didn't have a cell phone when I was eleven."

Fiona got up and carried the dirty plates into the kitchen. *But cell phones weren't even invented when you were my age,* Lizzy thought.

She unraveled her arms from her dad's neck and turned to her mom, who was sitting across from her, elbows resting on the table.

"Thank you, Mom," said Lizzy. "I promise to be responsible."

She couldn't wait to tell Cassandra.

Chapter 12

Lizzy hopped out of bed and hurried into the kitchen. *Where was everyone?*

"Hello?" she said, picking up the phone.

"Lizzy, it's me."

"Hi Cassie!"

"Are you hungry?"

"Definitely!"

While she was talking, Lizzy saw a note stuck to the refrigerator with a magnet. It was in Fiona's neat handwriting.

L: Walking Penny w J, be back soon. xo Aunt F

The red clock in the kitchen said 9:48 a.m. Then she remembered her dad had an early-morning doctor's appointment. Her mom had probably gone with him.

"I have an idea. Meet me in front," said Cassandra.

"Um, alright. I just need to get dressed really fast."

"Roger that."

"Who's Roger?"

"Never mind. I'll see you in a minute."

Lizzy threw on shorts and a T-shirt. On the bottom of Aunt Fiona's note, she quickly wrote in pencil, *Having breakfast with Cassie!* Then she left to meet Cassandra, careful to lock the door behind her.

"Have you been to Sammy's?" Cassandra asked when Lizzy got to her building.

She shook her head. "No, what's that?"

"It's the deli over there," she said, pointing across the street. "They have the best egg and cheese sandwiches in the whole world. And sometimes they give me free gum."

"Oh shoot, I don't have any money. My mom forgot to leave my allowance."

"Don't worry about the money. It's my treat!" said Cassandra. "I got twenty dollars for feeding Elvis, my next-door neighbor's turtle, so I'm rich! After we eat, we can go to Genovese to look for nail polish. You know, you can get three bottles for five dollars!"

They walked into the cluttered deli, its jam-packed shelves overflowing with canned food, boxes of cereal, and an endless supply of snacks. A gray cat napped in a warm spot of sun on the worn-out floor. A plastic fly catcher hung from the ceiling.

"We'll have two egg and cheese sandwiches on rolls. Thanks, Sammy!" Cassandra said to the short man with glasses working the grill.

"Coming right up. Hey, who's your friend?" he asked, gesturing to Lizzy, who was glancing at the packages of Twinkies and Hostess Cupcakes on the shelf by the cash register. Her mom never let her eat stuff like that.

"This is Lizzy. She just moved to the neighborhood. I told her how amazing your sandwiches are!"

"Hello there, Lizzy."

"Hi," said Lizzy, smiling. A few minutes later, their sandwiches were ready. Sammy passed them to the cashier, who didn't look much older than Cassandra and Lizzy.

"Thanks, Yusef. Can we also get two ice teas with extra sugar?" Yusef filled the cups with ice and pulled out a pitcher of tea from the refrigerator behind him. He packed everything up in a white paper bag, tossing salt, pepper and lots of sugar packets on top.

"Have a nice day!" Lizzy said, taking the bag.

"You too," said Yusef. Lizzy noticed he had crazy long eyelashes.

"Let's go to the playground," Cassandra suggested, stuffing the change in the pocket of her shorts.

McLean Park, on the corner of Nineteenth Street, was mostly empty on this humid morning, except for a teenage couple holding hands on the swings and three squealing toddlers running back and forth under the sprinklers as their babysitters watched.

The girls sat on a green bench across from the jungle gym. Lizzy unwrapped her sandwich and took a bite. The melted cheese oozed out. Cassandra sipped her iced tea and kicked off her sparkly silver flip-flops. Lizzy looked down at her old brown sandals and frowned. She wished she had worn her nicer ones.

"So how come you had to leave early from the Secret Club meeting? My mom said something happened?" Cassandra asked.

"Julian fell off his bed when he was jumping on it and cut his forehead head open. There was blood everywhere!" said Lizzy, extending her arms in the air dramatically. "He was hysterically crying. Sometimes when he gets that way, I'm the only one who can calm him down. I'm so annoyed I had to leave. Did I miss anything?"

"Oh no, poor Julian! The meeting was almost over anyway. We just ate more cookies and then people started to go. Walt and Chloe helped clean up."

"We went to the emergency room and Julian got a bunch of stitches, but he's fine now. He has a Band-Aid above his eyebrow."

"That's a relief. You're a good sister. So did you like the meeting?"

"Yeah, I had no idea what to expect and I was really, really nervous, but it turned out to be fun. Everyone was nice."

"Well, they all liked you, especially Walt."

"Really? I barely talked to him."

"I can tell. Plus, he texted me."

"Wait, he did?" Lizzy was shocked. But she wasn't surprised that Walt had a phone. Everyone did. "What did he say?"

"Just that you seemed nice."

"Oh." Lizzy wasn't sure what to do with that information. She decided to talk about something else. "So are you going to share next time?"

Cassandra looked at her for a second or two before responding. "Maybe. I like hearing everyone else's stories better."

Lizzy thought that wasn't really fair, but it was Cassie's club after all. She could do whatever she wanted, right?

"Who are the other Secret Club members?" she asked Lizzy, squinting into the late-morning sun.

Let's see, Amanda and Chloe go to Greystone with me. They're stepsisters. Chloe is in my grade, and Amanda is a year older. They live downtown and we take the bus together, but I wouldn't say we're like close friends or anything," said Cassandra. "Anyways, they won't be at any more meetings because they both just left for sleepaway camp for the rest of the summer."

She went on, "Josephine and I were in Girl Scouts together last year, but I don't do that anymore after I got in trouble because I didn't collect enough money from the cookies I sold. My mom had to write a check for the rest. She was so mad!"

"Yikes," said Lizzy.

"And Walt is my cousin. He lives near here. Actually, we're not real cousins. We just say that because our moms are best friends. He's going to share his secret next week."

"Wow!" Lizzy said. She felt a little jealous about all these people Cassandra knew, then she remembered what she said about Dylan Quinn and Hazel Leonard-Jones, Cassie's former best friend. Whatever happened, it must have been bad.

Lizzy took her last bite of egg sandwich and wiped her mouth with a paper napkin. "So, do you get along with your mom?" she asked.

"She's pretty strict. And she's super busy doing lawyer stuff."

"Sorry."

"But she is letting me be on my own this summer, as long as I get my work done."

"Work?"

"Yeah, chores and homework. Greystone has summer assignments."

"I would hate that."

"I like to read, and I really love doing math problems, so I guess it's not that bad. Hey, want to see if Walt is around? He's always playing basketball at the courts by the fountain. I bet you anything he's there right now."

"I should head back," said Lizzy, glancing at her watch. "My aunt is probably wondering where I am."

"Oh, come on, don't be such a goody-goody." She looked up, brown eyes pleading.

Lizzy took a deep breath and exhaled slowly. *What was her problem?* "Yeah, you're right. I guess I can hang out," she agreed.

Chapter 13

They left the playground, securing the metal safety gate behind them. Lizzy paused for a second and watched her friend walk a few paces ahead.

Cassandra wore cut-off denim shorts and a white tank top with flowers on the front. Her hair was piled up glamorously on top of her head. She was shorter than Lizzy with a different-shaped body. Lizzy was a straight up and down beanpole. And her hair was always a mess.

If Lizzy could borrow just a smidgen of Cassie's confidence, she'd be a happy girl. Cassandra moved through the world the same way she dove into the pool: like she owned it. As much as Lizzy wanted to find out what made Cassandra Reed tick, she would never come right out and ask. That would sound so pathetic.

Cassandra stopped, noticing Lizzy wasn't next to her. "Hello? Are you coming?"

Lizzy scurried to catch up and together the friends turned toward the drugstore. Just then, the sun tucked behind a cottony cloud, partially blocking its glare and cooling the air ever so slightly.

"So where were you born?" Cassandra asked.

"In a hospital."

"Very funny. I mean where, like geographically?"

"New Jersey. I've lived there my whole life," said Lizzy. "Until I had to move here, that is." She paused and looked over at Cassandra as they waited for a bus to pass. "Which I totally didn't want to do. No offense or anything. It's just that I loved Mount Olive."

"I get it," said Cassandra. "Moving sucks. I moved from Brooklyn to my apartment when I was four, but I don't really remember."

"You did? How come?"

They had crossed the busy street and were walking down the block to Genovese Drugs.

Lizzy made sure to step in the middle of each sidewalk square, not on the edges. In her head she recited, *Don't step on the crack or you'll break your mother's back*. She and Amy and Hannah always sang that during their walks into town to get ice cream at Hill's.

"That's where my grandparents lived. They helped take care of me when I was a baby."

"Do they still live there?"

"No, they moved away a few years ago to some town in Ohio."

"Do you miss them?"

"Nope." She answered so abruptly Lizzy was afraid to ask more. She shifted course. "What do you want to be when you grow up?"

"A movie star," she said without missing a beat. There was that confidence again. "What about you?"

"Well, I always thought I'd be an artist."

"You should! We need more creative people in the world. There are too many boring lawyers like my mom."

Lizzy chewed on her bottom lip. "Or maybe a doctor," she said.

"Well, you are good with emergencies. Like when your brother cut his head, am I right?"

"Yeah, I don't mind blood. I'm not one of those fainting types."

They kept walking. Cassandra swerved to avoid a pile of poop a dog owner had neglected to pick up. "Ew, gross!" she said.

Lizzy went on, "Actually, what I really want to be is a medical researcher."

"Make up your mind!"

"No, really. I want to find a cure for M.S.," she said softly. The girls had reached the drugstore with its blue neon sign. Flyers announcing sales on laundry detergent, toothpaste, and diapers crowded the front window.

"M what?"

"M.S. It's stands for multiple sclerosis." The words hung heavily in the air.

They made their way inside. Lizzy followed Cassandra across the ugly brown and yellow carpet to the cosmetics aisle at the back of the store. They continued talking by the nail-polish display.

"It's what my dad has."

Cassandra looked hard at Lizzy. "Seriously?"

"Yes." Lizzy chewed on her cuticle and stared at the metal buckles of her sandals. "He has trouble walking, and he gets really tired."

She paused. "There's no cure. My mom gives him a shot in his leg once a week, but I don't think it's helping."

Cassandra squeezed Lizzy's arm in a gentle way.

"The truth is, we moved to New York for my mom's new job *and* to make things easier for my dad. Our old house had too many steps."

"Wow, that must be hard for you."

"Sometimes, but I really try to focus on the positive." Lizzy didn't say how worried she felt all the time or how much she hated having a disabled dad.

"Well, I'm positive I love this color," said Cassandra, changing the subject. She held up a bottle of violet nail polish. "I'm buying it for you."

After checking out, they walked to the basketball courts and, lo and behold, there was Walt, standing to the side, guzzling from his thermos. He was facing away from Lizzy and Cassandra as they approached. Lizzy noticed the gigantic sweat stain on the back of his shirt. It was impossible to miss.

"Walter Blackstone, come to the principal's office!" shouted Cassandra in a fake English accent. Lizzy cupped her hand over her mouth to contain her giggles. Walt turned. When he saw them, he smiled and shook his head.

"Cassie, you need to work on that accent," he said, dropping his thermos onto the bench. Behind him, three older kids were playing horse at one of the other nets. Each time they made a basket, a chorus of "awesome shot, dude!" rang out.

"Whatever do you mean?" Cassandra said, still in the other voice.

"Because you sound like an American girl pretending to be a nutty British lady," Walt said, wiping his face with a black towel and plopping down on the bench, his long legs stretched out.

"What's up, Lizzy?"

"Hi Walt," Lizzy said, taking a seat on the bench. She pulled her inhaler from her bag and took a puff. The humidity was making her feel wheezy.

"You have asthma?" Walt asked.

"All my life. It's super annoying."

"Me too. But I always forget to bring my pump with me."

Cassandra stood in front of them with her hands on her hips. "So, Walt, did you figure out your secret?"

"Wait, when is that?"

"Tomorrow, remember I texted you? Can you make it?"

"I think I can. I just need to double-check that my mom doesn't need me to help with my grandmother," Walt said. "What about you, Lizzy?"

"I'm getting a phone today!"

"That's great," said Walt, "but I meant about the Secret Club."

Lizzy felt her face redden. "Oh right. Yeah, I'm coming. My aunt is making Rice Krispies Treats for us. They're to die for."

Cassandra lowered herself to a cross-legged position on the cool ground next to the bench where Lizzy and Walt were. Noise from the horse game continued in the background, along with the sounds of laughter and lively chatter from a group of girls playing hopscotch and jump rope.

"How's your grandma doing?" said Cassandra, looking down to examine her chipping toenail polish.

"Last time I saw her, she didn't even know who I was," said Walt sadly.

"Is she sick?" asked Lizzy.

"Yeah, she has dementia. Her brain doesn't work right anymore."

"Sorry, Walt," said Lizzy.

"It's okay. I'm going shoot a few more hoops before I call it a day," said Walt, standing up and grabbing the basketball from under the bench. "Get excited for the big reveal!"

"The big reveal?" asked Lizzy, confused.

"Yeah, that's when I spill the beans and tell my death-defying secret."

"Ooh, sounds dangerous," said Cassandra.

"Can't you give us a hint, Walt?" asked Lizzy. "Just a tiny one."

Walt pretended to zip his mouth shut and throw away the key.

"My lips are sealed!"

Chapter 14

"Can't Julian can stay here with Aunt Fiona?" Lizzy tried to hide her annoyance. Her little brother totally didn't need to go with them on this important errand.

"But I *want* to go!" Julian pounded his feet on the rug, accidentally kicking the dog's tennis ball across the floor. Penny sprang off the couch to retrieve it. "Daddy said we're going on an adventure."

Lizzy and Julian looked at their dad, who was stacking discarded newspapers and magazines from the week in a big pile on the coffee table. Next to him was a metal bin overflowing with cans and bottles.

"Before any decisions are made, you two need to take out this recycling. Now, please. You know the drill." Lizzy resisted the urge to roll her eyes at her brother. Instead, she pulled the shopping cart out of the hall closet, unfolded it, and proceeded to dump all the papers inside. Julian sulked.

Lizzy wheeled the heavy cart to the entryway. "Jules, hold the door for me like a big, strong boy." He just stood there staring into space, playing with the sleeve of his SpongeBob T-shirt, which was stained with chocolate milk from lunch.

"Wake up, Julian, come on!" At this rate, she would never get her phone.

Finally, her brother sauntered over. Lizzy unlocked the door and opened it.

"Just stand here," she directed. Julian's body prevented the door from shutting. Then Lizzy pushed the cart out of the apartment and down to the garbage room. "Follow me. Hurry, don't let the dog out."

But it was too late. As soon as Penny heard the commotion, she tore past Julian and took off down the hall as fast as her legs could carry her, the dirty ball clasped in her mouth. Julian ran after her, letting the door slam with a bang.

While Julian played catch with Penny, Lizzy deposited all the papers in the garbage room and then went back to retrieve the container of cans and bottles.

After what felt like an eternity, the recycling was in its proper place, and Julian and Penny were back in the apartment. Lizzy was anxious to get going.

"Dad, I did everything you asked, with no help from Julian, by the way, so can we please go now?" she asked, re-folding the shopping cart and stowing it back in the closet. "Just you and me, right?"

Their father was sitting at the dining table writing a list in green pen. His cane was next to him. So was Julian's stroller. Julian climbed in. "I'm ready!" he shouted, pumping his tanned legs up and down.

"I did tell your bother he could come with us," said their dad. "I have to pick up some things at the store afterwards, and you know how he loves Food Emporium." Lizzy's face fell.

Just then, Fiona came in from the other room. "Who wants to help me make cookies for dessert later?"

"I'm going with Dad to get my new phone! Or at least I'm trying to," said Lizzy, her hand on the doorknob.

"Me too!" said Julian. "I'm getting a phone like Lizzy."

"Um, no you're not, Jules. Three-year-olds definitely don't need phones."

"Do too."

"No you don't, but nice try. Stay here with Aunt Fiona and Penny, okay? Mommy will be home soon."

Julian was quiet as he weighed his options. Aunt Fiona sweetened the deal.

"Listen, Jules, if you help me with the cookies, you can watch a video before dinner. What do you think?"

Julian jumped out of the stroller and marched into the kitchen. Lizzy heard the refrigerator open. In an instant, her brother was back at the table, a roll of slice-and-bake chocolate-chip cookies in his chubby hands and a mile-wide smile on his face.

ξ

Even though it was only a few blocks away on Fourteenth Street, getting to the Verizon store took a long time. Lizzy's dad moved slowly, using his cane to steady himself. It took concentration to walk without losing his balance.

There were crowds of people passing them in both directions, and the sidewalk was uneven in places, slowing them down even more.

Lizzy tried to be patient, but it wasn't easy.

Maybe Julian should have come with them after all, she thought. Pushing the stroller always helped her dad walk better. And it was way less embarrassing. She took a sip of her water bottle as they turned the corner. *Why did she insist they go without him?*

"There's the Verizon sign up ahead, Dad!" Her heart pounded with excitement.

"Yup," said her father. "Almost there." He was tired. Once inside, he practically collapsed into a row of chairs by the door. Lizzy hoped no one noticed.

"What can I help you with today?" asked the energetic salesperson after Lizzy reached the front of the line. She motioned to her dad. He rose from his seat and slowly made his way to where Lizzy was waiting.

67

"I'm interested in a phone for my daughter," he said, placing one hand on Lizzy's shoulder and leaning against the counter for support. "But she doesn't need all the bells and whistles. Just a basic device for calling and texting."

"And music and games," Lizzy added. "Cassie told me there's a great app for playing Scrabble. We could play together!"

"I can show you several excellent models that are ideal for kids," the clerk offered. The name tag on his red Verizon shirt said "Charlie W."

Lizzy hoped her dad wouldn't ask a million pointless questions. "And if your daughter is on your family plan, you'll have the ability to monitor her activities and turn off any features you don't want."

After examining four different brands and listening to her dad ask close to a million questions, Lizzy settled on a compact white phone with a pink flowered case. While Charlie W. was busy activating her new device, her dad fished a credit card out of his wallet. She noticed his forehead was sweaty and his khaki shorts were wrinkled.

"Thank you, Dad. I love my new phone!" She held it like precious cargo.

"You're welcome, Murph. After dinner, Mom and I will go over the rules you'll need to follow. Got it?"

"Got it." Lizzy was beaming.

Lizzy imagined what her very first text message to Cassandra would say. She wanted to write something dramatic and unexpected, but in the end, she just wrote, *Hi Cassie! Guess who?*

Seconds later, Cassie texted back: OMG. *It's about time!*

Chapter 15

"Attention, everyone! Welcome to the fourth meeting of the Secret Club," announced Cassandra, standing in front of the common room in a blue-and-green sundress with spaghetti straps and a pair of navy-blue Converse high tops. Her hair was a cloud of tight black curls accented with a silver headband.

"Please turn off your electronic devices."

Lizzy pulled her new phone out of the front pocket of her jean shorts and fumbled around until she figured out how to silence it by pushing the button on the side. She hoped no one noticed how lame she was.

Along with Walt and Lizzy, only two other kids showed up, a new girl in a Harry Potter T-shirt and white cropped pants named Abby and a boy with an olive complexion and dark silky hair. Lizzy thought she kind of recognized him, but she wasn't sure from where.

They helped themselves to Aunt Fiona's Rice Krispies treats and lemonade. Lizzy passed out paper napkins. Abby used one to blow her nose.

"Lizzy, look who I convinced to join our club," said Cassandra, her arm around the shoulder of the boy with the dark hair. He looked more nervous than she was last time. It felt good not to be the newest member.

Staring at his face, Lizzy suddenly remembered: He was Yusef from the deli! Cassandra must have used her powers of persuasion to convince him that the Secret Club was nothing short of amazing.

It was hard to say no to Cassandra. She had a way about her, that was for sure. Being pretty didn't hurt either.

As she took attendance and introduced everyone, Cassandra acted like Little Miss Serious. Lizzy tried to break her concentration by sticking out her tongue and crossing her eyes, but Cassie just tapped her Snoopy pen against her clipboard and called on Walt.

"This may surprise some of you, but I'm like the biggest basketball fan there is in the entire universe," he began. "I spend a lot of time watching games on TV and shooting hoops at the park. One day last summer, when we were visiting my aunt and uncle at their house upstate, it was raining cats and dogs, so my brother, Spencer, who is almost as tall as I am, and I decided to play one-on-one in the family room downstairs. We moved the couch out of the way and used a laundry hamper as the basket. What could go wrong?" Walt asked. Lizzy laughed out loud.

He went on, "Spencer made a shot and I blocked it with my whole body. The ball flew across the room and smashed into a shelf with my uncle's bowling trophies. Fortunately, my aunt and uncle weren't home at the time because it made a gigantic crash. We put everything back, but his one trophy – the first place something-or-other with a gold guy holding a bowling ball – broke apart. Instead of fessing up, we Crazy Glued the two pieces back together and hoped no one would notice. And they never did."

Grinning, Walt sauntered back to his seat next to Lizzy, while everyone clapped. "Terrific story, Walt!" said Cassandra. "Abby, are you ready to share?"

"That was great!" Lizzy whispered to Walt.

The small, pale girl made her way to the front.

"Hi, I'm Abby," said the girl, staring off into the distance. "My secret is, one time when I was in fourth grade, I forgot to do my math worksheet, so I copied all the answers from my friend Suzanne's paper and handed it in. I got an A." She sat back down without uttering another word. *That was short and sweet,* Lizzy thought. She smiled at Abby and mouthed "good job."

Then it was Yusef's turn. He was shaking like a leaf. Playing with the hem of his gray T-shirt and shifting from one sneakered foot to the other, he began reading from a page in a loose-leaf notebook.

My Secret

What would you do if you had a cat named Secret?

Would it always hide away?

What would you do if your secret was a kite?

Soaring above the clouds

What would happen if your secret was misunderstood?

Like the end of a game of telephone

My secret starts with S and ends with T

The rest is a mystery to you

But not to me.

Everyone sat in stunned silence. Lizzy was pretty sure her mouth could catch a fly or two. Breaking the spell, Cassandra jumped up and started applauding. The rest followed.

"Wow, Yusef, you are a super great poet," said Cassandra, wrapping her arms around his neck.

"Yeah, that was fantastic," Lizzy added.

"Thanks," Yusef answered quietly.

Then Cassandra said, "I have something to share." No one was expecting Cassie to share anything, least of all Lizzy.

She turned to face her audience, lifted her chin up, opened her hands like a starfish, and cleared her throat dramatically. She was practicing being a movie star, after all, Lizzy reminded herself.

"When my ex-best friend Hazel decided she didn't want to be my friend anymore because Dylan Quinn was way cooler, I said something I kind of wish I hadn't," began Cassandra. Lizzy was intrigued.

She continued, "It happened after the fifth-grade concert. We were hanging out in front of Greystone waiting for our parents to pick us up when..." She paused. "Actually, I can't tell you. It's a secret."

"Come on, Cassie! We all shared our secrets!" said Walt.

"Yeah!" added Lizzy helpfully.

"It's my club and I can do whatever I want."

Lizzy wanted to strangle her.

Chapter 16

"Lizzy! Breakfast! I'm not going to call you again. Now come on!" said her mom. Lizzy crawled out of bed and shuffled to the table in her slippers.

"Aunt Fiona was nice enough to take the dog out for you earlier, even though it was your turn. I guess you needed your rest, huh?" her mom said, barely containing her impatience. Lizzy wished she liked coffee because she needed some right now. Instead, she downed a big glass of orange juice.

"Why are you so tired?" her mom asked. "Didn't you sleep well?"

"I woke up in the middle of the night," said Lizzy. "I don't know why."

The truth was, Lizzy had stayed up late emailing her friends from home on her mom's laptop, but she didn't want to tell her mother that. She had only gotten one email from Hannah since she moved. Only one! And none from Amy. *Had they actually forgotten about her already?*

"Sometimes herbal tea helps me when I can't sleep," said her mom. "I'll make you a cup tonight."

"Okay, thanks. Where's Dad?" asked Lizzy, looking around the room.

"He was still snoring when I got up. He must be awake by now."

Her mom, wearing a light-blue terrycloth bathrobe, stood at the stove flipping blueberry pancakes in a black pan.

The table was set with cloth napkins and the dinner plates usually reserved for special occasions. A pitcher of maple syrup and a small dish of butter rested in the center. Aunt Fiona was working her magic again, Lizzy thought, as she surveyed the tidy apartment.

"Hi Aunt Fiona, the place looks great! And thanks for walking Penny."

"You're welcome. Remember, your mom's starting her new job tomorrow."

"Oh right," said Lizzy. "Do you have your outfit picked out, Mom?"

"I have no idea what to wear! Maybe you could help me later?" she said, turning from the stove to glance at Lizzy.

"Sure, when I get back from Cassie's." She started texting Cassandra.

"Lizzy, no phone at breakfast. Let's not get into a bad habit, okay?" With a sigh, Lizzy put her phone back in her pocket.

As her mom stepped aside, Aunt Fiona removed the steaming plate of pancakes from the oven with a pair of orange potholders. "Ooh, these smell delicious," she said.

"How's my baby boy?" Lizzy sang to her brother, who was sprawled on the couch watching cartoons. Below his dark bangs, a pink Hello Kitty Band-Aid covered his stitches.

"I'm not a baby!" Julian protested, stamping his stocking feet on the floor for emphasis.

"Sorry, how's my big boy?"

"Ah, there you are. I was beginning to wonder," said their mom, turning to greet Lizzy's dad as he came in from the other room, his hair wet from the shower.

"Hi, everyone. I guess I'm little slow this morning. Probably just need some of Mom's pancakes and I'll be good as new," he said with his usual optimism.

Holding on to the walls, her dad slowly walked toward them. He leaned with all his weight on the edge of the table to pivot his body into a chair, but his right

74

hand slipped. Without the strength to support himself, he fell to the floor. Lizzy watched helplessly as her mother and aunt rushed over to him.

Two glasses and a plate slid off the table and crashed. Luckily, her father wasn't hurt, but it took all their might to lift him up and into the chair. Lizzy felt scared by all the commotion, although she kept her feelings quiet.

"Daddy! Daddy!" shrieked Julian, throwing his arms around his father. "Why did you fall down?"

The next few minutes were a swirl of chaos. Lizzy took Julian into her room and tried to keep him occupied, but she could still hear her mom and aunt's urgent voices.

"He's burning up," her mom said to Aunt Fiona.

"I'm calling 9-1-1," said Fiona, reaching for her cell phone.

"Cal, honey, can you hear me?"

Lizzy opened the laptop and clicked on an episode of *Sesame Street*.

"I'm scared," said Julian. He started to cry. Lizzy pulled him closer and hugged him tight. "Daddy's going to be fine, Jules. He just needs a doctor to look at his boo-boo, like you did when you cut your head," she said. But she wasn't so sure.

Lizzy plugged in her headphones and popped the buds in her brother's ears. Cookie Monster sang a silly song on the screen, distracting Julian.

Soon, the screaming sirens of an ambulance grew closer. A minute or two later, the buzzer rang, followed by forceful knocking. She could hear people talking in the living room and banging and rustling sounds. She opened the door a crack to see her dad being strapped onto a stretcher and her mother reaching for her purse. Lizzy's heart was racing. She couldn't catch her breath.

Was her dad going to die?

Chapter 17

The elevator slid open. Aunt Fiona and Lizzy walked off onto the seventh-floor patient unit, which was illuminated by bright fluorescent lights.

Over the intercom, a woman's voice paged Dr. Jasper Allen to call the 7W nurse's station. Another shouted something Lizzy couldn't make out. The air smelled like Lysol, hamburgers, and pee all mixed together. It made her feel kind of queasy.

Lizzy's mom greeted them, her frizzy hair escaping from a messy ponytail. She looked tired in her wrinkled dress and running sneakers. She held a small notebook in her hand.

"Mommy!"

Lizzy's mom hugged her so close Lizzy could smell her breath.

"How's Daddy? What did the doctor say? Is he coming home soon? When will he feel better? Can I see him?" Lizzy's questions poured out in a nonstop stream. She worked herself into such a state that she started wheezing.

"Let's take your puff-puff, sweetie. We don't need two family members in the hospital," said her mom, placing an arm around Lizzy's shoulders.

Lizzy pulled her inhaler from her pocket and expertly administered two puffs of albuterol, holding her breath for five seconds in between each. Her mother rubbed her back until her breathing steadied.

"Are you better now? Oh my poor baby," her mom said, stroking Lizzy's cheek. "Where's Julian? He didn't come with you, did he?"

"I called George and Audra—they came over to watch him. They're going out for ice cream," said Lizzy's aunt.

"Okay good." She looked back at Lizzy. "Daddy is doing well. I just met with Dr. Williams, and he was encouraging." *Encouraging about what?* Lizzy wondered.

Her mom continued, "Now let me chat with Aunt Fiona quickly, then we'll go to Daddy's room. Can you sit here for just a minute? We'll be right back," she said, pointing to a chair by the bank of elevators.

Fiona blew Lizzy a kiss before she and her mom moved a few steps away to talk. Lizzy turned her head toward their muffled voices, straining to hear. Her mom was reading from her notebook. Aunt Fiona listened intently.

Lizzy's bare arms and legs shivered with goosebumps from the hospital's air conditioning. She wished she had brought her sweatshirt.

Only two family members at a time were allowed in the patient rooms. So Aunt Fiona rode the elevator to the basement cafeteria in search of iced coffee, and Lizzy and her mom walked around the corner to the 7 West unit.

Lizzy was eager to see her dad, but she felt nervous too. Hospitals were scary places. What if they couldn't make him better?

"Hi Daddy!"

"There's my best girl!" Her father was sitting up in his bed, picking at a tray of baked chicken, mashed potatoes, and something that looked like it could have been a vegetable in a past life.

A dingy plaid curtain divided the room in two. His roommate, an old man recovering from some kind of operation, was snoring on the other side.

Lizzy hugged her dad tight, careful not to disturb the tubes coming out of his arm. Her mom leaned over and gave Cal a kiss. "How's my favorite patient? Our daughter is ready to entertain you!"

"Yeah, Dad," Lizzy chimed in. "I brought books for us to read and the crossword puzzle from the newspaper and a pack of playing cards and my sketchbook. I thought I could draw a picture for you."

Aside from his uncombed hair, a hideous blue hospital gown, and the two I.V.s secured with white tape to his arm, Lizzy thought her dad looked mostly like himself, maybe a little tired. That was until she looked down at his left leg, which was elevated by two pillows.

"Pretty angry looking, huh? Don't worry, Murphy, I'm getting pumped with lots of good stuff," said her dad, gesturing to the see-through bags dangling from a metal pole.

The lower half of his leg, from kneecap to the base of his bandaged foot, looked like it had the worst case of sunburn ever. The limb was a red that resembled the inside of a summer tomato and was swollen to nearly double its normal size.

Although she felt sorry for her dad and everything he was going through, Lizzy wasn't grossed out by medical stuff like some of her friends were. She found it fascinating.

She hoped her dad would let her give him his nighttime shot someday. Right now, her mom was in charge of that.

"What's this line for?" Lizzy asked, leaning in for a closer look. Along the edge of his leg, just below the kneecap, there was a dark pen mark. Someone at the hospital must have written on his skin for a reason.

"That shows where the infection started when I got here this afternoon," her father explained. Lizzy noticed the redness had already extended a few inches above the blue line, toward his thigh, kind of like water rising in a measuring cup. When she touched his leg, it felt weirdly warm.

What if the infection kept going and never stopped? What would her dad do then? Her heart sank.

"Lizzy, I'm going to check on Aunt Fiona. My texts aren't going through. Keep a close eye on Daddy and make sure he doesn't get into any trouble," her mom said, winking, as she squeezed her daughter's arm.

"Okay, Mom. I'll try. Want to play cards, Daddy?" She started to shuffle.

"Only if you promise not to cheat!" Her dad yawned loudly.

Just then, a plump older woman wearing burgundy scrubs came in pushing a small machine on wheels. Her name tag said "Jackie Diaz, R.N."

"Time for your vitals, Mr. Zander," she announced, wrapping a blood-pressure cuff around her father's upper arm and sliding a thermometer under his tongue.

"Oh, hello there," the woman said when she saw Lizzy sitting in the visitor's chair. "Are you helping take care of your daddy?"

"Yes. I'm Lizzy."

"Well, nice to meet you, Lizzy. You look just like your mom."

"Thanks." Lizzy smiled. She got that a lot. It was probably because they both had red hair.

The machine beeped. Nurse Diaz read the thermometer. "101.2. He still has a fever," she said. "The Tylenol should kick in soon. And your blood pressure is 100/72." Her dad had closed his eyes.

"Is that good?" Lizzy asked, putting the playing cards on the table.

"Yes, your dad has a strong heart." She released the Velcro cuff from his arm.

"But what about his leg?"

"That's what this medicine is for," said the nurse, pointing to one of the hanging bags. "That's a powerful antibiotic. It's going to kill the bacteria so your dad's leg can heal."

"Oh. What's it called?"

"Amoxicillin. You know, you should think about studying medicine when you get older. I can tell you'd be a natural."

"I want to be a researcher, to find a cure for M.S.," said Lizzy.

"That's wonderful. I am sure your dad is very proud of you," she said.

"I also want to be an artist."

"Wow! An artist. Is that what all these pretty pencils are for?" She pointed to the metal box next to Lizzy.

"I'm making a drawing for my dad. Of me and my little brother."

"He could use a little decoration in this room, that's for sure."

Lizzy nodded.

"Looks like your dad's getting some much-needed shut-eye," she said, lowering her voice and nodding toward the bed. She snapped off her latex gloves.

Lizzy looked over at her dad. He was sleeping soundly, his chest rising and falling with each breath. It felt weird watching him.

"I'll check in later," Nurse Diaz said. Bye for now, Lizzy." She wheeled the machine down the hall.

Lizzy pulled a light-green pencil from the box and started sketching.

After a few minutes, her mom came in carrying a cup of coffee with a plastic lid on top. "Come on, sweetheart, time to go home. Aunt Fiona is waiting for us in the lobby."

Lizzy brushed her teeth and crawled into bed, pulling her quilt up to her chin and curling on her side, the way she liked to sleep. She was exhausted. After a few minutes, her mom came in and sat on the edge of the bed, stroking Lizzy's hair.

"Sorry it was such a hard day, honey," she whispered. "I'm proud of what a brave girl you were in the hospital."

"Why did Dad get sick? Is it because of his M.S.?" Lizzy had turned to face her mother.

"He has an infection caused by unhealthy bacteria. A little cut or scrape can allow bacteria to enter anyone's body, even Penny's, but having M.S. does make Daddy more susceptible to getting sick."

"I'm scared he won't get better."

"Oh baby, he will. I promise. He's getting the absolute best care. Now try to sleep. Tomorrow's another day. I'll be with Daddy at the hospital again. You're welcome to come along or stay here. Aunt Fiona will be taking Julian to day care in the morning, then to get his stiches out."

"I'll stay here. But can you call me or text me to let me know how Dad's doing? I may want to visit later on."

"Of course. Good night, sweetie." She kissed the top of Lizzy's head.

"Mom?"

"Yes, honey?"

"What about your new job? Won't you get into big trouble if you don't go tomorrow?"

"Family comes first, Lizzy. Always. My company will understand. I already called them." She slid out of the room. Lizzy could sense how anxious her mom was. She felt so bad for her.

Chapter 18

The next morning, Lizzy fixed herself a bowl of cereal. She poured milk over the corn flakes, sprinkled blueberries on top, added a spoonful of sugar and stirred. She thought about what she wanted to do with her day. She was still so worried about her dad.

Penny growled at the sound of keys jangling outside of the door. Lizzy looked up to see Fiona coming in, wearing a wide-brimmed straw hat over her braided hair and a dress with rainbow stripes. The dog jumped up to greet her.

"Hi puppy! Who's my good girl?" said her aunt, walking into the kitchen and helping herself to a glass of water from the pitcher in the fridge. She had just returned from dropping Julian off at Big Apple Kids.

"And how's my favorite niece?" she said. She took a sip and looked into Lizzy's serious face. "It's been a rough few days, huh?"

Lizzy nodded. She was afraid she'd burst into tears if she tried to say anything.

"I know how hard this is for you." *But you don't understand,* Lizzy thought. *No one does.*

"I know," Lizzy said. Her voice was barely there.

"Listen, I'm taking Jules to the doctor to get his stitches out later this afternoon. It won't be a big deal, just a few little snips, but maybe you want to come? To take your mind of things."

Lizzy stared at her cereal in the red bowl for what felt like a long time. The air conditioner buzzed in the background. Penny scratched her ear, rattling the clasp on her collar.

"Your corn flakes are getting soggy, sweetie pie." Aunt Fiona put her arm around Lizzy and held her close. "Why don't you join us?"

"Thanks, but I have stuff to do here. I'm almost done with the drawing for Dad. And I want to visit him again." She took a bite of corn flakes. A spot of milk dropped on to her chin. She swiped it away with the tip of her finger.

"I know he'll love your picture, Lizzy," Aunt Fiona. "Your dad's lucky to have so much love in his life, and you and Jules and your mom are a big part of that. Remember, he's going to get better. You just have to be patient and let his body work its magic."

"Okay." She took another bite. The mushy cereal tasted gross.

"If you want to see him, I'll take you to the hospital before I pick your brother up. How does that sound?"

"Good. Thanks Aunt Fiona." Lizzy dumped the rest of her breakfast in the garbage and rinsed her bowl out in the sink. She knew she'd be hungry later but right now she didn't feel much like eating.

"I'm going to take a shower," she said.

"Good idea. Try my peppermint shampoo. It's in the orange bottle."

Lizzy went into her room, changed into a robe, and texted Cassandra.

Can u talk?

Yup!!!!

I'm calling u.

K

"What up?" answered Cassandra. "Is everything okay?"

"No," Lizzy said, her voice shaking. "My dad's in the hospital."

83

"What? What happened?"

"He has a bad infection on his leg. I meant to text you last night, but I fell asleep. It was like the worst day ever."

"Is it because of his M.S.?"

"Maybe, I'm not sure. My mom said he's more susceptible."

"What's that mean?"

"It means he has a better chance of catching germs, I think."

"Oh. Do you want to come over? We can make popcorn and paint our nails."

"Thanks, but I'm about to jump in the shower," said Lizzy. "Then I think I'm going to visit my dad. You know, to give my mom a break."

"Text me later?"

"I will."

"Hope he feels better."

"Thanks, Cassie."

After her shower, Lizzy got dressed and wrapped a towel around her head. She sat down on her bedroom floor and leaned her back against her bed. Determined to finally finish this drawing, she opened her sketchbook and her box of pencils and got to work coloring in the rest of Julian's features.

She had already drawn what was supposed to be her face. She wasn't so sure it looked anything like her, but she did find the perfect red for her hair.

As her picture came to life, Lizzy tried to relax. She stretched her bare feet out in front of her and wiggled her newly painted toes.

Subject : Hi !
From : elizamurphyzander@gmail.com
To : amyyvonnekim@gmail.com

Hi Amy,

84

Sorry I haven't written in a while. Things have been so dramatic! My dad is in the hospital!!!

He has C E L L U L I T I S, which is a skin infection all over his leg caused by bad bacteria. I had to ask my mom how to spell it.

My mom was supposed to start her new job the day after my dad got sick, but she couldn't. She called them up and said she needed to start a week later because it was an emergency.

I'm so glad Aunt Fiona is staying with us. She's the best!!

OMG! Big News: I got a phone!!! When you get yours, we can text all the time!

I hope you haven't forgotten about me!

Love 'til the ocean freezes,
Me

Chapter 19

Entering the huge lobby of New York University Medical Center, Lizzy looked up at the color-coded signs. She checked the scrap of paper in her pocket. "Mom said to follow the green path to 7W. But I don't see..."

"There's the green circle, Lizzy, over there," Her aunt pointed to a passageway on the left of the lobby, next to the gift shop.

They headed in that direction. At the end of the corridor, Lizzy pushed the up button for the elevator. "You don't have to come with me. I know where to go. Mom's already up there."

"I'll just ride up to the seventh floor with you, alright? Then you can walk to your dad's room by yourself. Deal?"

"I guess so." In the elevator, Lizzy double-checked the contents of her tote bag: two books, the newspaper, her dad's favorite music magazine, playing cards, her inhaler, her art supplies, her water bottle, Rice Krispies treats wrapped in foil, and her drawing, which Aunt Fiona had rolled up nice and tight and secured with a rubber band.

"Go straight down this hall, got it? Now give me a hug. Love you, sweetie."

"Thanks, Aunt Fiona. Take a photo of Jules getting his stitches out, okay?"

"I promise. Wait, hold on, you ate lunch, didn't you?"

"Yup, I had the leftover spaghetti from the fridge when you were doing your yoga," said Lizzy. "Can I please go now?" She was eager to see her dad and mom.

"Yes, yes, go on," said her aunt.

Knowing Aunt Fiona was watching, Lizzy walked toward 7W. She passed people in scrubs rushing in and out of rooms and a few patients in baggy gowns circling around the unit. One, an elderly woman with bright-red lipstick, held on to an IV pole as she chatted in another language to a younger woman.

When Lizzy got to her dad's room, his bed was empty. Her mom wasn't there either. A plate of untouched food rested on the tray table, next to a pink plastic water pitcher.

His reading glasses were on the tray, too, and the menu for the next day and a yellow pencil. The curtain in the middle was pulled closed. Lizzy guessed her father's roommate was on the other side, but she couldn't hear anything.

Lizzy sat in the brown guest chair and took out one of her books. She opened it up to her bookmarked page and tried to focus on the words, but it was impossible to concentrate. She checked her watch—2:05 p.m.

She pulled her phone out of her pocket.

Mom where r u?

Then she licked her lips and ran her tongue over her front teeth. She unsnapped her barrette and fluffed up her hair with her hands. She tied her sneakers a little tighter. What if something bad happened? Did her mom forget she was coming? Another look at her watch – 2:11 p.m.

Finally, the voices Lizzy heard in the hallway grew closer. "Here we are Mr. Zander." Relieved, Lizzy turned to see a tall man in dark-blue scrubs pushing her dad in a wheelchair. Her mom was right behind them.

Lizzy ran to hug her dad. "Daddy! I have your drawing! You can hang it up next to your bed. It's of me and Jules."

"Thanks Murphy," said her dad slowly. It sounded like he was underwater.

"Sorry hon! Dad had to get a test on his leg," said her mom, rushing to embrace Lizzy. "We thought we'd be back before you got here. Are you okay?"

"I texted you," she said quietly.

"The wi-fi is terrible in the hospital, so it probably didn't go through." She looked at her phone. "I didn't get a message from you."

The man in the blue scrubs was trying to lift her dad back into bed. Another worker came to help. Lizzy noticed that his gown had fallen off his shoulder and his leg was still super red and swollen. He didn't seem like himself at all.

"I think we're in the way, Lizzy," said her mom. "Why don't we step outside for a minute while Daddy gets settled?"

Lizzy grabbed her tote bag and followed her mother a few doors down the hallway to the family lounge.

"Mom, he looks really sick." She sat down on the hard couch and took a drink from her water bottle. Her eyes filled with tears.

Her mom held her hand. "Dad had to wait a long time for this test, and now he's tired. But I talked to Dr. Williams earlier and he said dad is responding well to the new antibiotics. The first drug wasn't strong enough. Which means he's definitely on the mend. It's just going to take a little longer."

"What was the test for?"

"They wanted to check his circulation, to make sure the blood is flowing through his leg properly. We should get the official results in a little while, but the technician said she didn't see anything abnormal."

"That's good, right?" asked Lizzy.

"Yes, very good."

"Mom?"

"What is it, hon?"

"Do I have to go to swimming tomorrow?"

"Well, it's up to you, but I think it's is a good idea. Exercise helps relieve stress. I told Ms. Olsen I'm joining the class!" Lizzy's mouth fell open.

"I'm kidding, sweetheart," she said, squeezing her hand.

Lizzy made a face at her mother.

"Is this your drawing for dad?" her mom asked, touching the rolled-up paper poking out of her bag.

Lizzy nodded. "Want to see?"

"Let's find out what Daddy thinks." She stood up, smoothing the front of her skirt and pushing a piece of hair behind her ears. "Come on."

Lizzy's dad was resting comfortably in his bed, flipping channels on the TV. His leg was wrapped in gauze and elevated. An IV dripped medicine into his arm. His lunch was gone, except for a cup of melting vanilla ice cream and a sliced orange.

"Hi Daddy! Open your picture!" She handed him the tube of paper.

Her dad took the tube from her and tried to pull off the rubber band to unfurl the paper, but he struggled. Lizzy couldn't believe how weak he was.

"Here, let me help you," said her mother, gently opening up the drawing of Lizzy and Julian. "I'll go ask for some tape to hang it up," she said.

"I love it," was all her dad managed to say before he drifted off to sleep again.

ξ

Lizzy's dad was in the hospital for most of the next week. Her mom visited every day, and Lizzy came once more. She read a chapter of their book out loud to him and tried to play a game of Go Fish, but after less than an hour, he was worn out.

She felt frustrated and sad.

89

"We're going to story hour at the library," said Aunt Fiona, as she wiped peanut butter off the table. Julian was such a slob, but weren't all three-year-olds?

Lizzy had just gotten back from spending the night at Cassandra's, which was fun, but she couldn't stop thinking about her dad. She texted her mom four times. Would he ever leave the hospital?

"Why don't you come along? We can stop at Frosty's on the way back."

"Yeah! Frosty's! Can we go right now?" yelled Julian. He had a pink scar above his eyebrow, but his bangs mostly covered it up. "We can get some ice cream for Daddy and put it in the freezer!"

"Great idea, Jules, but after the library, okay? And let's use our inside voice, please," said their aunt.

Julian crossed his arms and pouted. "Don't you want to hear Miss Clover's stories?" asked Fiona, playfully pinching Julian's cheeks. "Now go wash your hands and face in the bathroom. Come on, hurry up now." He skipped down the hall.

Miss Clover, one of the children's librarians, acted out the books with lots of energy, making believable voices for each character. Julian adored her.

"I'm going to stay here," said Lizzy.

"All right, kiddo, if that's what you want to do," said Fiona, steadying the stroller while Julian hopped in. "We'll be back in an hour or so."

"Have fun," said Lizzy. She went to reorganize her colored pencils, trying to stay busy.

Twenty minutes later, her phone rang. "Hold on a sec, sweetie. Someone wants to talk to you," her mom said. Lizzy could hear beeping noises in the background.

"Hi Murphy!"

"Daddy!!!" Lizzy was thrilled to hear her dad's voice. He sounded more like himself. "How are you feeling? When can I come visit you again?"

"You don't need to," said her dad. "I think I'm finally getting kicked out! My leg is better. I still have to take antibiotics but the pill kind. No more tubes in my arm. I'm done with all that."

"For real?"

"For real. I can't wait to see you and your brother. I love you so much!"

"I love you too, Daddy!"

Lizzy hung up and jumped in the air. Her dad was coming home!

ξ

That night, they ordered Chinese food from the place next to McLean Park. It was Lizzy's idea. She had their egg rolls once when she was at Cassandra's and thought they were delicious.

"We have to get more than just egg rolls, Lizzy," her mom said as she studied the menu on her laptop. "Let's see, how about moo-shoo pork and chicken and broccoli?"

"Broccoli is yucky," cried Julian.

"Get something with tofu, too, Mar," Aunt Fiona chimed in.

"And something extra for Daddy to eat, like that shrimp thing he likes," suggested Lizzy as she leaned over her mother's shoulder to look at the screen.

"This? Hot and sour prawns?"

"No, the one with garlic and those green beans," said Lizzy.

"You mean snow peas? Okay, I'll get that. Are we all set? I'm checking out." Lizzy's mom fished her credit card out of her wallet and clicked the keyboard a bunch more times. "Done. It'll be here in half an hour. Plenty of time to set the table and pour the water."

When their dinner arrived, Lizzy's family took their usual seats at the table—Aunt Fiona next to Lizzy, Julian across from them in his booster seat, their mom on one end. Penny perched on the other chair, her nose in the air. Chances were good that she'd get a little something before the end of the meal.

"Don't get too comfy," said Lizzy. "That's Dad's chair." The dog just stared with her dark eyes.

"Can I show Daddy my boo-boo?" asked Julian. He lifted up his hair to reveal his fresh scar and the tiny dots where the stitches used to be. A half-eaten egg roll sat on his tray in a circle of soy sauce.

"Of course, Jules," said their mom. "He's getting discharged tomorrow morning. Sometime after ten, they told me. You can see him when you get home from day care."

"Yay!" said Julian, pounding on his tray.

"Julian was such a brave boy when Dr. Washington took his stitches out. Weren't you, buddy?" said Aunt Fiona. She picked up a piece of broccoli with her chopsticks and popped it in her mouth.

"It didn't hurt," said Julian. "I wanted to go back to school after, but Aunt Fiona wouldn't let me."

"Because it was dinner time, sweetie, remember?"

"Jules, what do you like best about Big Apple Kids?" asked Lizzy as she scooped a helping of the chicken dish onto her plate.

"Choice time! Want to know why?" His blue eyes widened with excitement.

"Why?" asked Lizzy.

"Because there are lots of horses to play with!" He dipped the rest of his egg roll into the sauce and took a bite, chewing a mile a minute.

"Slow down, Julian. You don't have a train to catch," said their mom.

He swallowed and continued talking. "And in music Mr. King is showing us how to play the ukulele."

"Wow, Jules, that's great. What's a ukulele anyway?"

"You don't know what a ukulele is? Lizzy's joking, right, Mommy?" Julian looked up at their mother for reassurance.

"Yes, your sister is teasing you, honey." She shot Lizzy a look. Lizzy rolled her eyes. "But, Jules, I thought lunch was your favorite activity because you like to eat so much. You're a little porky pig! Oink! Oink! Oink!"

"I'm not a pig. Mommy, make her stop!"

Chapter 20

"Mom, what's all this?" Lizzy asked as she grabbed the two bulging shopping bags from her and put them on the kitchen counter.

She started to unpack the bags: fried chicken and collard greens; meatloaf and mashed potatoes; and warm bagels with containers of cream cheese, smoked salmon, and cucumber salad.

"We have to fatten Daddy back up," said Lizzy's mom. "He's nothing but skin and bones after being in the hospital. The bagels are for lunch and the rest is for later. Hey, why don't you invite Cassandra over for dinner?"

She was slicing bagels with a long knife and arranging them on a plate. "There's enough food for an army."

Even though she knew Lizzy's mom and Julian and Penny, Cassandra hadn't met Lizzy's dad, and she had never been over to Lizzy's apartment. Lizzy almost always went to Cassandra's place since there was so much more room or they met up in front of their buildings. It was just easier that way.

"I guess I could," said Lizzy.

"You don't sound very excited," said her mom.

"I don't know if she can. Sometimes her mother doesn't let her do things."

"It was just a suggestion, Lizzy," said her mom. "Can you go see what your brother is doing? Tell him we're about to eat."

"Sure."

What if her dad lost his balance when Cassandra was here and fell? Or dozed off at the table, which he sometimes did after taking his medicine? That would be so embarrassing.

Lizzy was mad at herself for feeling this way, but she couldn't help it. She wished she didn't care what other people thought.

After going back and forth in her mind, she decided to invite Cassandra.

Can you come for dinner? she texted.

A few minutes later, Cassandra replied with a smiley face.

Lizzy spent a few hours re-reading *From the Mixed-Up Files of Mrs. Basil E. Frankweiler*, one of her favorites, and drawing a new picture. Finally, at 5:30, the buzzer rang. Lizzy jumped to answer it.

"Hi!" she said Lizzy, giving her friend a big hug. "I love your outfit!"

Cassandra was wearing a jean skirt and a white blouse with a round collar. Her curly hair was in two ponytails, tied with pink ribbons, and her earrings were round purple studs that looks like candy. Lizzy wished her mom would let her get her ears pierced.

"Thanks! My mom made me dress up."

"Ha! My mom would do the same. Let's go to my room." Penny barked a few times but calmed down once she recognized Cassandra.

"This is for you." She handed Lizzy the paper bag she had in her hand.

Lizzy dumped out the contents on to the bed. Three bottles of nail polish with white tops tumbled out. She examined each label—"Ballet Slippers," "Jelly Donut," and "Metallic Madness."

"Ooh, I love these! Thanks so much. How much do I owe you?"

She was glad she decided to invite Cassandra over and not just because of the nail polish.

"Nothing," said Cassandra. She was lying on the floor of Lizzy's room, looking up at the ceiling. "You can buy the egg sandwiches next time."

"I'm glad your mother let you come. I guess you finished your homework?"

"Yeah, mostly. My mom was in a good mood for some reason. Your room is really cute. It's like a little dollhouse room."

"Thanks. I wish I had a big room like yours."

"This is much cozier. I love all your drawings." Cassandra scanned the papers hanging on Lizzy's walls. "I could never draw that well, not in a billion years."

"But you're a fantastic swimmer. And you can do super hard math problems in your head!"

"True. I guess we all have things we're good at. I'm good at eating, too. When's dinner?"

"Let's find out." They walked into the living room. The adults were talking loudly, nearly drowning out the background music. Julian sat on Aunt Fiona's lap, playing with the stack of beaded bracelets on her wrist.

"Hi Cassie!" he said. "Want to play Connect 4?"

"Of course, Julian. If you promise to let me win!"

"Aunt Fiona, this is Cassandra," Lizzy said.

"Well, hello! It's a pleasure to finally meet you, Cassandra." She put out her hand for Cassandra to shake.

"Thanks for helping my girl get used to this big city. She needed a friend like you," said Aunt Fiona. Lizzy gave her aunt a look that said, "stop embarrassing me."

"And this is my dad," said Lizzy, turning to her father, who was sitting on the couch, his cane tucked out of the way.

"Hi there!"

"Nice to meet you," said Cassandra. "Look at all these records," she remarked, admiring her dad's enormous music collection, which was stored in old milk crates along one wall of the living room. "Which one's your favorite, Mr. Zander? My mom loves Aretha Franklin."

"That's a tough one," he said. "I guess you could describe my tastes as 'eclectic,' which means I like a little bit of everything. When I was in the music industry, I got to go to concerts all the time. There's nothing like live music."

"Cool!" said Cassandra. "So, you work for a record company? That's what Lizzy told me."

Lizzy felt heat rising in her face. She bent down and pretended to tie her sneaker.

"I used to work for one of the major record labels, but not anymore," he explained and gave her a kind smile.

"Oh," said Cassandra.

"Girls, how do you feel about taking Penny out before dinner? I think her bladder's about to burst," said Fiona, coming over with the dog's leash. Penny scurried around their feet, her tail wagging wildly.

"Make it quick because dinner's almost ready. We're just warming up the meatloaf," her mom reminded them.

The girls walked around the block, stopping here and there to let Penny sniff around.

"You must be happy your dad is feeling better," said Cassandra.

"Yeah, so happy. We're really close."

"I can't believe how many records he has! I didn't think people had records anymore. My mom only listens to Spotify."

"He's old-fashioned, I guess, and totally obsessed with music." Lizzy paused, biting her lip. "But he doesn't work anymore. You know, because of his M.S. I know I said he worked for a record company, but he doesn't. Because he can't."

"Hold the phone, Lizzy, she's pooping!" Cassandra shouted suddenly. Just then, Penny squatted down to do her business smack in the middle of the sidewalk.

"Uh oh, I forgot a bag!"

"Are you kidding? We can't just leave it here for someone to step in!"

"Wait, Cassie, let's see if there's something over there we can use." They walked to the garbage can and looked inside.

"How about this?" said Lizzy, reaching in and pulling out a torn sheet of newspaper.

"Go for it! I'll wait here," she said, grabbing Penny's leash."

Just then, a skinny woman walking a big black poodle rounded the corner. Penny growled. Cassandra sprang into action.

"Excuse me! Ma'am?" she said. The woman turned. "We have a little emergency. Would you happen to have an extra bag we could borrow?"

"Here you go," the woman said, handing Cassandra a green plastic bag from her purse.

"Did you actually say 'borrow'?" said Lizzy after the woman walked away. "Like you were actually going to give it back?" The friends erupted in laughter.

Chapter 21

The following Saturday, Cassandra called to invite Lizzy to the movies. *Toy Story 4* was playing at the Village Theater. They were both dying to see what Woody and Buzz were up to this time.

"My mom needs my help with something this morning, but I'll be home later." Lizzy twirled her fingers around a piece of her hair. She could smell bacon sizzling on the stove.

"Lizzy, time for breakfast," she heard her aunt say. "Off the phone please."

"It's at 4:00," said Cassandra.

"Can we get popcorn?"

"Obviously!"

"Lizzy, now!" said her dad.

"I gotta go, Cassie. I'll text you later."

"Later gator!"

She joined her family at the table, helping herself to a handful of strawberries from the bowl in the middle. They were from the farmers market and so delicious.

"Thanks so much for coming with me, Lizzy," said her mom. She sipped her mug of coffee. "It shouldn't take too long."

"That's good because I want to go to the movies later."

Lizzy had agreed to help her mother move into her new office. She was determined to hit the ground running, especially since she was starting a week later than planned. Plus, they hadn't spent much time alone these past few weeks, with everything that had been going on.

After he finished eating, her dad put his plate on the floor. In a flash, Penny licked it clean.

"And you say *I* spoil the dog? Seriously, Dad?" said Lizzy.

"What can I say? She just loves scrambled eggs," said her father, shrugging his shoulders.

"She loves all food!"

"Go get your shoes on, Lizzy. Best to wear sneakers. And don't forget to put sunscreen on," said Lizzy's mom. "Julian, you and Daddy are in charge of doing the dishes! Aunt Fiona needs a break."

"I am not doing the dishes!" Julian protested.

"Yes you are, superstar!" said their dad. "Then we can have some fun!"

Best Friends United was on East 49th Street, near Grand Central train station. The animal adoption center was on the first floor, and the hospital and offices were higher up in the white stone building.

Lizzy and her mom took a yellow cab to get there. If it weren't for the two boxes of stuff they had to carry, Lizzy would have made her mom ride the bus.

As far as public transportation went, Lizzy liked to stay above ground. She hated the subway, even though she had only ridden it a couple of times. It was dirty and smelly and boiling hot. Worst of all, everyone was mushed together like the mountain of socks in her overflowing drawer.

After signing in at the security desk, her mom escorted Lizzy to the seventeenth floor, through a set of glass doors, to a medium-size office, where a brand-new desktop computer sat on an L-shaped desk, next to a tall metal filing cabinet and a pair of bookshelves. As far as she could tell, they were the only people there. It was so quiet.

"Here we are!" said her mom.

"Wow, I love your view!" Lizzy stared out one of the windows. The people walking along the sidewalks below looked like ants.

"Here, help me empty these, Lizzy."

Her mom pulled the packing tape off the top of the cartons, which she had stacked on the carpeted floor, and lifted the flaps. Lizzy had fun organizing the framed family photos on her mom's desk and arranging the books, knickknacks, and potted plants on the shelves under the windows.

— Lizzy —

With the hammer and nails she brought from home, her mom hung two of Lizzy's drawings—one of bare trees against a bright winter sky and the other an action shot of Penny catching a tennis ball in her mouth—on the wall opposite her desk so she could always see them when she looked up. She also hung a collage of a clown that Julian created in his old nursery school.

"Why did you pick those?" Lizzy asked.

"Because I love them, and they remind me of you and your incredible talent."

Lizzy smiled. "Are you excited to start your new job, Mom?"

"Yes, but I'm a little apprehensive, too. I'm not sure what to expect, especially because I'm starting later than planned."

"Really?" Her mom always seemed so confident.

"Grown-ups get nervous too, Lizzy. Everyone does at some point or another. It's part of life."

"I know. I'm nervous about school," she said, looking down at her hands.

"I know you are, sweetie. And that's completely to be expected. Once you meet your teachers and connect with a few of your classmates, you'll feel a lot more relaxed. I promise."

"I hope so."

"By the way, Lizzy, I'm proud of you. Daddy and I both are."

Lizzy didn't say anything. Her mom went on. "I know what a challenging summer it's been for you, adjusting to a brand-new city, and then with Dad in the hospital. It's been a tremendous amount to deal with." She swept a strand of hair from Lizzy's face.

"I'm glad you and Cassandra have become good friends. She's a nice girl, and I like seeing you happy."

"Thanks, Mom, but I still miss Hannah and Amy." A moment passed. "Is Daddy better now? What if he has to go back to the hospital?"

Her mother's eyes were soft. "I don't want you to worry about your father. He's doing well. And the last thing he would want is for you to spend a single second worrying about him. Now let's finish up here so you can enjoy the rest of the afternoon."

As instructed, Lizzy stomped on the empty boxes to flatten them and stowed the hammer in her mom's tote bag. She switched off the office light and followed her mother down the hall to the elevator.

"What do you think your brother and Dad are up to?" Lizzy's mom asked as they rode the bus back downtown. She took her phone out of her purse to text Lizzy's dad.

The bus driver had to take a detour near Madison Square Park because there was a street fair blocking Broadway. Lizzy could see the crowds of people from the window.

"Julian is probably making Daddy play horses or Operation," Lizzy said.

"No, he likes playing Operation with you more because you're so into medical stuff."

"Yeah, that's true. Maybe they're just watching *Sesame Street*. Jules can't get enough of Cookie Monster."

Lizzy couldn't believe how fast Julian was growing up. She adored her little brother and was embarrassingly proud of him, although sometimes she missed his long-gone fat cheeks, toothless grins, and sweet baby smell. And now he had a scar on his perfect forehead!

The next major milestone was potty-training—Lizzy was more than happy to leave that one to her mom and dad.

Chapter 22

By the end of July, Lizzy and Cassandra had become inseparable. Her dad teasingly called them "The Dynamic Duo."

They swam together at the Y, went out for French fries at the diner, bought egg sandwiches at Sammy's, and spent hours walking around the neighborhood, ducking into air-conditioned stores along the way to cool down. Sometimes they stopped at the basketball courts to watch Walt.

Lizzy didn't know what would happen in September once they started at different schools. Right now, she considered Cassandra her best friend. Of course, she'd never tell Hannah and Amy that.

"I can't believe you've never read *The Outsiders*," Lizzy said. "It's only the best book ever!"

They were walking to the library after swim class. It was an overcast afternoon, with gray clouds in the sky. Lizzy hoped it wouldn't rain because she'd forgotten to bring her umbrella.

"Well, what about *Are You There, God? It's Me, Margaret?*" Cassandra shot back. "Judy Blume is the best writer. She understands what it's like to be a girl becoming a woman, if you know what I mean. And it takes place in New Jersey!"

"She gets her period, right?"

"Yes, but it's about way more than that. You have to read it, Lizzy, so you'll be ready when Aunt Flo comes."

"Who's Aunt Flo? I have an Aunt Fiona but no Aunt Flo."

"Not yet, but you will. We both will, not that I'm in a big hurry or anything."

"Oh, I get it. Duh." Lizzy scrunched up her face. "Can't wait for that!"

"Anyway, I'm trying to decide when we can have the next Secret Club meeting. A lot of people are away," said Cassandra. "My mom and I are going on vacation next week."

"You are?"

"Yeah, to the beach. We go every year. It's kind of boring. My mom won't let me text or email. She says it's an 'unplugged' vacation. Whatever."

Lizzy didn't want to think about Cassandra being out of touch for a whole week. "Walt's secret last time was hilarious!" she said, changing the subject.

"I can't believe his uncle never found out that his trophy was held together with Crazy Glue! And I'll never get over Yusef's poem. Who knew he was such a great writer?"

"Just because he works at this father's deli doesn't mean he's not smart or creative."

"I know," said Lizzy. Maybe she had thought that.

They strolled to the corner, glancing around at the construction projects that seemed to be everywhere. Did the city really need more buildings? Lizzy lifted the hair off her sweaty neck.

"Are you going to finish sharing your secret or are you going to leave us hanging?" Lizzy asked. "I want to find out what happened with Hazel and Dylan!"

"I doubt it. That's not my only secret anyway." Cassandra said as they stepped off the curb. *What was she talking about?* Lizzy wondered.

"But I thought you created this club so everyone could share their secrets."

They stopped walking. Lizzy looked into her friend's brown eyes, which were framed by flower-shaped earrings and two twisted ponytails, the latest in a series of inventive styles Cassandra pulled off flawlessly. Lizzy's hair would never look that terrific.

"I tried to share, but it's too hard," she said, her voice rising. She turned and bolted into the library, leaving Lizzy standing alone on the sidewalk.

Chapter 23

Lizzy sat cross-legged on her bed and stared out the window. Even though there wasn't much to see—just a red-brick wall that blocked the sunlight — she focused her eyes in that direction anyway and thought about some things that had been on her mind her lately.

She wondered, did she actually miss her old friends or just the idea of them? Sometimes she believed they were the only ones who truly understood her, at least the Lizzy she used to be.

Hannah and Amy cracked up at her silly jokes and sought her advice about very important matters, like whether Hannah should try out for the fifth-grade track team (she did) or become a vegetarian (she didn't) or if Flynn Vaughn had a crush on Amy or just flashed that huge smile at everyone? (Turns out, he was extremely friendly.)

They asked how her dad was doing and spoiled Julian with tons of hugs and an endless supply of gummy bears. And Hannah and Amy always knew if Lizzy was upset or annoyed or about to explode with some earth-shattering news simply by the expression on her face.

For example, Lizzy was the first to find out that Mrs. Lloyd was pregnant last fall and Miss Westlake, the mean substitute they all hated, would be taking over for four whole months, a fact she tried, and failed, to keep from her friends.

It didn't help that Lizzy's face turned fire-engine red and her freckles seemed to darken in response to her emotions. Whether she was laughing or crying or so mad she wanted to scream, her face gave her away.

Up until a few days ago, Lizzy would have said Cassandra totally understood her too, that she was her best friend, the person she cared the most about and who cared the most for her. But now she wasn't so sure.

Did she really know Cassandra? Come to think of it, did she really know herself? Who was Eliza Murphy Zander?

Lizzy pulled her spiral notebook from her backpack and turned to an empty page. At the top, in purple pen, she wrote:

11 THINGS ABOUT ME! (with a squiggly line underneath)

And then she created this list:

1. Turning 12 on November 4th!
2. Red Hair and Freckles (Ugh)
3. I love to draw!
4. I love Oreos
5. I love my brother Julian and my dog Penny and, of course, AUNT FIONA!!!! (with another squiggly line)
6. Moving to New York was hard
7. My dad has M.S.
8. ~~Sometimes I am afraid he will die.~~ She immediately crossed this out.
9. What if no one likes me at my new school????
10. Does Cassandra have a secret?
11. I need new Lip Smackers!!!

There was a knock at the door. Startled, Lizzy tore out the page and crumpled it up in her hand. The purple pen rolled on to the floor.

"Come in?"

The knob turned, and the door opened. In walked Aunt Fiona, her crazy auburn hair unbraided and spilling over her shoulders like a lion's mane.

"Hi kiddo, this came in the mail for you." She handed Lizzy a big white envelope. When she saw the return address—School of Tomorrow on East Twenty-Fourth Street—she felt instantly disappointed.

"Oh, thanks," she said flatly, tossing the envelope with the smiling globe on to the floor.

"I have to pick up some things at the drugstore. Want to come? There may some new nail polish for my favorite niece!"

"Um, I'm your only niece, so don't I have to be your favorite?"

"You got me there. But, if you have something better going on, I'm sure my favorite nephew would love to tag along." Fiona gave her a mischievous grin.

"No, don't take Julian! I want to go! He can stay here with Daddy."

"Okay then, get your shoes on. We're leaving in five minutes."

Fiona exited the room, shutting the door behind her. Lizzy opened her hand and looked at the ball of paper in her pink palm.

She fully intended to toss it in the wastepaper basket—after all, it was just some dumb stuff she wrote down—but at the last second, she stuck the paper in her dresser drawer underneath a stack of neatly folded underwear.

She and Aunt Fiona strolled down the block in the direction of Genovese Drugs. Even though it was late in the afternoon, the air still felt uncomfortably hot and sticky.

Within seconds, the underarms of Lizzy's T-shirt moistened with perspiration, and her hair morphed into a disheveled mess. Aunt Fiona had the good sense to re-braid hers before heading out into the humidity.

"I'm going to miss you, Lizzy."

"Me too." Lizzy was surprised by the sudden lump in her throat. She felt tears behind her eyes but vowed not to embarrass herself by crying like a baby in public. She would rather eat eyeballs.

Still, she couldn't believe Aunt Fiona was actually leaving. Couldn't she stay longer? Couldn't she live with them forever and ever, or at least until Lizzy went away to college in seven years?

Or how about this: Lizzy could move to Montana with Aunt Fiona and then she wouldn't have to go to School of Tomorrow.

Montana had to have much friendlier middle schools, Lizzy was sure of it. And she could draw and do yoga and....

"I know you're sad. I'm sad, too. Really sad. You know why?" Aunt Fiona's voice brought Lizzy back to reality. Enough daydreaming.

"Why?"

"Because spending all this time with you has been a gift. An amazing gift. You, my dear, are a beautiful girl, and I am so proud of you."

They had arrived at Genovese Drugs, which, to their relief, was air conditioned. They were talking in the feminine hygiene aisle.

"Um, it's kind of awkward standing here surrounded by all this stuff," Lizzy said, gesturing to the boxes of tampons and pads.

"Oh sorry, I just need to get some supplies for the trip home. Doesn't your mom use this brand?" asked Fiona, holding up a blue box of Playtex tampons. "Wait, you haven't gotten yours yet, have you?"

Lizzy wanted to die. "Oh my God, Aunt Fiona, can we please go?" she whispered before bolting off to the relative comfort of the magazine aisle, where she picked up a copy of *Seventeen* magazine—the Back to School issue!—and turned its glossy pages.

After they finished shopping, Aunt Fiona treated Lizzy to ice cream at Frosty's. Lizzy considered her mint-chip cone with rainbow sprinkles the least Fiona could do for her after that completely mortifying visit to the drug store, plus the bottle of tangerine-sherbet nail polish Fiona let her pick out, of course.

"I admire you, Lizzy," said Fiona, who was digging into her dish of rocky road with a white plastic spoon. They had found a spot at one of the outside tables.

"What do you mean?"

"You are brave and kind and you never give up."

"I'm not brave. I'm a scaredy-cat."

"Don't be silly. I see how you handle hard situations—like your dad's M.S. and when he was in the hospital. And moving to this big city. That couldn't have been easy for you."

Lizzy licked her cone so the melting ice cream wouldn't drip down her arm.

She watched the passersby: two women in sundresses pushing strollers; a man walking a huge reddish-brown dog with floppy ears, who was panting heavily in the heat. She remembered her mom explaining that dogs don't have sweat glands, so they cool down with their tongues, a fact she found very intriguing.

Next, two girls maybe a little younger than Lizzy, wearing matching short overalls and baseball caps, crossed in front of her table, laughing at something. Lizzy thought they looked like twins.

"And you're a terrific artist, Lizzy," Fiona continued, pausing for a moment to toss her empty dish into the nearby trash can.

"You see the world with an artist's eye. Your drawings are stunning. If you keep at it, your work could be exhibited at famous museums!" Lizzy bit into her cone with a crunch.

"Hey Lizzy." She turned to see Walt standing on the sidewalk, cradling a worn basketball in the crook of his arm. A red-and-white thermos dangled from his other hand. He was crazy tall.

"Oh hi, Walt. This is my aunt, Fiona. This is Walt, Cassandra's cousin. We met at her ... apartment."

Lizzy almost forgot her promise to keep the Secret Club secret from grown-ups. Cassandra's mom knew it was some kind of summer activity her daughter organized for her friends, but she didn't know about the secret part. That would ruin everything.

"Hi Walt, it's so nice to meet you," said Fiona. "Want to join us?" Lizzy gave her a look.

"I'm just heading home from shooting hoops and really need to take a shower. Believe me, you wouldn't want me sitting next to you right now! No siree!"

"Do you live near the basketball courts?

"Yup, over on Twenty-Second Street, just past Fifth. Not far from my new school."

"You have a new school?"

"Yeah, I'm going to School of Tomorrow. It's on Twenty-Fourth. I'll be in seventh."

"No way! I'm going there too. Starting sixth grade." Lizzy tried to tone down her enthusiasm. She couldn't believe Cassandra didn't tell her.

"Well, we need to get going too. See you around, Walt."

"Catch you on the rebound!"

Lizzy waved as Walt turned the corner and disappeared into the afternoon.

Chapter 24

Lizzy was getting ready for swim class when her phone beeped. A text from Cassandra.

I need to talk to u!! I'm out front, can I come up?

Sure!

Lizzy hadn't spoken to Cassandra since that day at the library last week. They exchanged a few texts but about nothing important. She wasn't sure what to expect.

Moments later, the buzzer rang. As always, Penny started barking like a maniac, convinced a robber was about to break in.

When Cassandra came through the door, she looked like she had been crying. Her usually perfect hair was a tangle of disorderly pieces around her face. Her earlobes were bare.

It was obvious she had gotten dressed in a rush: Her striped T-shirt was on inside-out, and her flowered shorts didn't match. Penny sniffed her sneakers and walked away, unsatisfied.

"Are you okay? What's going on?" Lizzy was worried. *Did something terrible happen? Maybe she got her period?*

"Is anyone here?"

"My mom's still at work and Julian's at daycare. But my dad is in my parents' bedroom. He's probably listening to music or reading so he's not going to hear us. Why? You're scaring me, Cassie."

"Do you have any food?"

"Want an ice cream sandwich? Or, wait, my mom just bought a new box of Oreos, unless my brother ate them already..." Lizzy opened and closed the cabinets as she talked. Cassandra stood there, staring into space.

Lizzy pulled the box down from its spot behind the saltines and grabbed the milk from the fridge and two mugs.

Shutting the door behind them, Lizzy and Cassandra settled onto Lizzy's bed, leaning their backs, which were cushioned by a pile of soft pillows, against the wall. Penny was banished to the other room to wait for the rest of the humans to come home.

They ate their Oreos and drank their milk for what felt like forever.

Finally, Cassandra spoke. "I just had a big fight with my mom. I hate her." She sounded like she might start crying again. Lizzy reached for her box of tissues, just in case.

"What happened?"

"I was watching the Food Network in the den in my pajamas and painting my toes during the commercials. She came home from work early. I didn't finish the list of things she left for me to do, and she freaked out and screamed at me and acted like a lunatic."

She paused to take in a breath. "I was supposed to water her millions of plants and take the trash out and fold the sheets and towels that were piled in the laundry hamper. I was planning to do every single thing, but she came home before I could. She called me lazy and said I didn't care about anybody but myself."

Her voice was shaking. "That made me so mad, I wanted to scream. I told her I didn't want to live with her anymore, that I was going to move in with my father. Then I ran down the hall to my room and slammed the door. She's so mean!"

Lizzy struggled to make sense of what her friend was saying.

"Your father?"

"He lives in Albany. I'm sure I'd be happier living with him. I doubt he yells like that."

Lizzy was speechless. She thought Cassandra's father had passed away when she was a baby, that's what Cassandra told her when they first met.

She knew Cassie and her mom had their share of arguments, but why in the world would she want to do something like that? It just didn't make sense. And why would she lie about something this massively huge?

"What are you talking about?" said Lizzy. "Your father's alive?"

Cassandra just stared at her, not saying a word. Finally, she nodded her head.

"Wait, I don't understand. I thought..."

"I just said that because he doesn't want me anymore. I have to go." She left Lizzy's apartment without saying goodbye.

Chapter 25

"Hey Daddy, want a smoothie?" Lizzy called out, waving a ripe banana in the air.

Trying to keep herself occupied, she had already re-arranged her closet, sorted her Lip Smackers by flavor, made a card for Hannah's birthday next week, washed all of Julian's horses and lined them up in a row on the floor of his room and made her parents' bed, taking extra care to fluff up the pillows the way her mom liked them.

She even cleaned the Westie salt-and-pepper shakers with a Q-tip. Now she turned her attention to her dad.

"Wow, Murphy, you're really on a roll. What's next? Giving Penny a bath?"

"I'm just doing stuff to keep busy."

Her dad was sitting on the sofa next to the kitchen, his latest book resting on his lap. He still had a few more pounds to gain to get back to his weight before he was in the hospital. He did love those protein smoothies, even though they smelled like dirty socks.

"Well, if you insist on fattening me up. I'll have extra peanut butter, please!"

"Coming right up!"

Lizzy filled the blender with a handful of ice, two heaping spoonfuls of crunchy peanut butter, a scoop of protein powder, and the peeled banana. Penny waited patiently to lick the spoon.

Lizzy pushed the on button and the machine sprang to life, causing a racket. After a few deafening seconds, she switched it off and poured the thick, brownish liquid into a tall glass and stuck in a straw. Then she joined her father in the living room.

"Thanks! This is even better than the ones Mom makes for me."

"Because she one-hundred-percent skimps on the peanut butter."

Lizzy settled into the rocking chair and put her bare feet on the oval coffee table, a move her mother wouldn't allow, but her dad didn't seem to mind.

He wore old gym shorts and a blue T-shirt that said "NYC" in an animated red apple on the front. Only her father could get away with wearing a corny shirt like that without looking like a tourist. His hair was sticking up on top, and week-old beard stubble covered his face.

Although his cellulitis was completely healed, and his leg looked like a normal dad leg, Lizzy couldn't help worrying that the bad germs would come back again

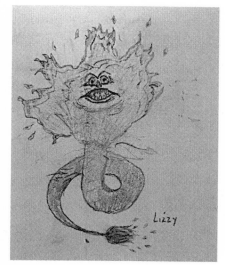

and make him sick.

One night when she was having a hard time falling asleep, Lizzy drew a monster that she imagined had inhabited her father's leg, with snarling, razor-sharp teeth, bulging eyes, and a body formed from volcanic flames. She didn't show the picture to anyone. Instead, she folded it into quarters and stuck it in the back of her sock drawer.

"What can I do to make you feel better?" asked her dad, abandoning his book and tossing it on the couch.

After her peanut butter treat, Penny snored on the carpet next to her chewed-up tennis ball and one of Julian's crayons that had somehow escaped from the toy box.

"Nothing. I'm fine."

"You don't seem fine. First of all, you're a cleaning machine. This is not normal Eliza Murphy Zander behavior." He got up and walked to the kitchen, dragging his foot along the tiled floor. A news program played on the radio.

"I told you, I'm just staying busy."

"It seems like maybe you're avoiding something? Or someone?" Lizzy wasn't in the mood to talk to her father right now, especially not about Cassandra.

"I'm okay, Dad. Really. I'm going to take a shower."

Lizzy kissed her father on the cheek and headed into the bathroom, a pink towel draped over her arm. Washing her hair with the peppermint shampoo Aunt Fiona left would probably make her feel better, at least for the time being.

"Please don't take too long," her dad called after her. "I told Mom when she texted earlier that we'd start dinner before she and Julian got home. We're having turkey burgers and fries."

Lizzy wished she had the nerve to call Cassandra. She was still her friend, wasn't she? Maybe if Cassie explained everything to her, it would make sense. Her feelings were a jumbled web of questions and confusion. Why was everything so complicated?

After rinsing her hair until the soapy water ran clear, Lizzy turned off the faucet, and stepped out into the steamy bathroom. Pulling on her robe, she tied her hair up in the towel, and rubbed Vaseline Intensive Care all over her freckled arms and legs. She hated having such dry skin. Sometimes she felt more like a reptile than an eleven-year-old girl.

Subject : Hi !
From : elizamurphyzander@gmail.com
To : hannahbanana99@yahoo.com

Hi Hannah,

Everything is B. A. D. This is why:

Aunt Fiona went back to Montana! I miss her so much. On the plus side, the apartment doesn't feel so crowded, and Julian started sleeping in his own bed!

Remember I told you I thought Cassie was keeping something from me? It's true!! AND she totally lied. She told me her dad died when she was a baby but he didn't. She made the whole story up!

I don't know who to trust anymore!

Are you excited for your birthday???? I'm sad we won't be able to celebrate together.

Love 'til the ocean freezes,
Me

P.S. Guess what else? Walt goes to School of Tomorrow! Another thing Cassie didn't tell me.

P.P.S. Did your parents say yes to the phone yet???

ξ

Lizzy was unusually quiet during dinner. "Earth to Lizzy!" her mom said. "Are you with us?"

"Yes, Mom," Lizzy responded, absentmindedly swirling a French fry in a pool of ketchup.

"Why don't you tell us about your day. I see you were very productive. I'm impressed. The place looks great."

"Thanks."

"What else did you do?"

"I made Daddy a smoothie that he said was way better than the ones you make." She smiled at her father. "Can I be excused?"

"We're still eating, Lizzy," said her mom. "This is family time."

"Please? I have to do something."

"What's so important?"

"I want to look at my School of Tomorrow stuff. To start getting ready," she lied. Her parents traded glances.

"Clear your plate and put it in the sink," her dad reminded her. "And please give Penny a scoop of food and some fresh water before you vanish."

Later, after Julian was asleep and her parents were in their room reading, Lizzy soundlessly opened the front door and walked out.

She dialed Cassandra's number. If her parents realized she wasn't home, she'd be grounded for at least a century, but this was important.

"Hi stranger," Cassandra answered.

"Hi! Guess what? I snuck out. I'm calling you from outside!"

"Wow! Maybe you're not such a goody-goody after all."

"Can you meet me?"

"Come to my lobby. I'll be down in a sec."

"No!" said Lizzy, practically shouting. "I don't want Malcolm to see me. He may say something to my mother."

"Doormen never snitch. He has more important things to worry about than what two twelve-year-old girls are doing on a boring summer night. Besides, he's probably listening to the Yankees game on his radio. We could steal the T.V. and all the furniture from the common room and he probably wouldn't even notice."

"I'm only 11.9 but whatever."

"Seriously, Lizzy?"

"Never mind, I'm on my way!"

Lizzy marched next door.

"Hi Malcolm," Lizzy said as sat down on one of the sofas. Cassandra was right: He was glued to his pocket radio and barely nodded in her direction.

A minute later, Cassie appeared wearing striped pajama pants, an oversized T-shirt, and slippers shaped like teddy bears. Her hair was in a curly ponytail on top of her head.

"Hi," said Cassandra.

"Hi. I like your slippers."

"Thanks. I got them for Christmas last year. They're super comfy."

"I can't stay long because my parents will completely freak out if they find out I'm not home. I wanted to say I'm sorry."

"Why are you sorry? I'm the one who lied to you."

"Because of your dad. You said he didn't want you. I couldn't imagine my father not wanting me." Lizzy met Cassandra's eyes and smiled.

"Someday I'll tell you the story, but for now, no more secrets."

"No more secrets."

"You'd better run home, or you'll turn into a pumpkin. I love you. I don't deserve such a great friend." Cassandra gave Lizzy a hug and turned toward the elevator.

"I'll love you until the ocean freezes!" Lizzy called after her.

"Huh?" Cassandra spun back around.

"Oh, sorry, I made that up a long time ago, before I met you. It means until the end of time. Because the ocean will never freeze, get it?"

"That's so cool. I'll love you until the ocean freezes, Lizzy Zander."

Chapter 26

"Hi Lizzy!" Lizzy's mom said when she answered the phone.

"Hi Mom."

"What a nice surprise. How's my darling daughter?"

"Pretty good. I'm at Cassandra's. How's your day?"

"I'm a little sad. Arlo was just diagnosed with leukemia, which is a kind of cancer. He's about to start chemotherapy. It's hard to know how he'll respond."

Arlo was a sweet calico cat with orange paws, orange-and-black markings and white on the tip of his tail. Abandoned as a kitten, he had lived his whole life at Best Friends. The staff and volunteers all spoiled him. He was her mom's favorite (aside from Penny, of course), even though she said she loved all the cats and dogs at Best Friends equally.

Visiting the animals in the shelter on the first floor gave Lizzy's mom a break from her stressful job upstairs, which made her a happier person at the end of the day, at least that's what she told Lizzy.

"Poor Arlo."

"Maybe you can come see him."

"Yeah, maybe." Lizzy paused and took a breath. "Mom, Dad fell again. I thought you'd want to know."

"Lizzy, why didn't you say something before? I'm going on about the cat. Never mind. It doesn't matter. Tell me what happened."

"Cassandra was at the dentist for her cavity, so Dad offered to go to the library with me to look for new books. When we were walking back, all of a sudden, he wasn't next to me. I looked down, and he was on the sidewalk. I think maybe he tripped over his cane or the curb or something."

"Oh dear. He wasn't hurt, was he?"

"He cut his knee and scraped his hand a little. These two people passing by helped him up. When we got home, I cleaned his leg with alcohol like you showed me and put a Band-Aid on it. He called me Florence something or other, whoever that is."

"Nightingale. Florence Nightingale. She was a famous nurse. I'm sorry, sweetheart. Dad is lucky you were there."

"I guess. Why does he keep falling? Is his M.S. getting worse? Is it because it's so hot and humid outside?"

"Let's talk about this when I get home, all right? Please don't worry about Daddy. It's almost time for my staff meeting, so I have to dash. I love you, Lizzy. Say hello to Cassandra. You girls have fun!"

"We will. Bye Mom. Love you, too."

Lizzy hung up and went to find Cassandra. Entering her den, she saw that she had created a picnic. A green beach towel with white diamonds covered the floor.

On top of that, Cassandra had arranged a spread of food: a plate of ham and Swiss-cheese sandwiches cut into squares, a bowl of potato chips, a dish of Oreos, and two cups of sweet iced tea.

"You did all this?" asked Lizzy.

"Yup, what do you think?" said Cassandra, extending her arms.

"I love it! You're the best!"

They settled onto the towel.

"What's up with your mom?"

"I called to tell her that my dad fell. Again."

"He did?"

"Yeah, it's been happening a lot lately. Last week he lost his balance in the bathroom and my mom and I had to drag him into the bedroom, so he could pull himself up on to the bed. It's like his legs don't work anymore." Lizzy sipped her tea and took a bite of a sandwich.

Cassandra stared at her. "That must be scary."

"I wish my dad didn't have M.S. It's not fair."

A moment passed.

"I wish I had a dad like yours," said Cassandra. "He's so nice and funny. I like how he calls us The Dynamic Duo." Lizzy smiled.

"Hey, what's the story with your father? Remember you were going to tell me?"

"Oh, right. All I know is he rode a motorcycle and played guitar. My mom met him at a camp in upstate New York. They both worked there. She was only twenty-two when I was born, and they broke up right after. My grandparents helped raise me in Brooklyn when I was little. My mom said they didn't like my father because he wasn't black."

"Wow," Lizzy whispered, not sure what else to say.

"I have my mom's brown eyes and wild hair. I wish I looked more like my dad. He had lighter hair and big green eyes, kind of like yours," she said, studying Lizzy's face. "Are you going to eat that last Oreo?"

"No, I'm stuffed. You can have it."

"I can't believe our last swim class is tomorrow already." asked Cassandra. "I know how much you're going to miss Ms. Olsen!"

125

"Ha ha! I'll never be her favorite, like you are," said Lizzy. "Actually, she ended up being not terrible. I learned a lot."

"And you got so much better! Remember how awkward you were when you first learned how to dive?"

"I'll never forget 'curl toes, tuck head, bend knees, and spring forward'! That will be stuck in my head forever, thanks to Ms. Olsen."

"Are your parents coming tomorrow?" For the showcase?"

Ms. Olsen had a kind of open house on the last class of the session. Parents and caregivers were invited to drop by to watch the swimmers demonstrate their aquatic skills.

"I forgot to ask them," said Lizzy. The truth was, she didn't want them to come. She knew her mom would be too busy with her new job, and it always made her nervous when her dad was out in public. She never knew if he would trip or lose his footing.

Plus, unlike Cassandra, she hated to be the center of attention.

ξ

Later that night, Lizzy volunteered to give Julian a bath and get him ready for bed. She had been so preoccupied with Cassandra and all her drama that maybe she had neglected her brother a tiny bit. They hadn't read together or played horses in what felt like a million years. She missed him.

"Knock, knock." Julian said. He was reclining in the warm tub, shiny white soap bubbles floating all around him like a magical snowstorm. His shampoo-covered dark hair formed an alien-like cone on top of his head. His scar had faded to a thin pink line.

An assortment of plastic toys joined him in the tub, bobbing on the surface or hiding somewhere under the water. Julian's curious hands kept finding random items – a few horses, a little boat, the empty barrel and five or six monkeys from Barrel of Monkeys (where the others disappeared to was anybody's guess), a squeaky caterpillar that belonged to Penny and definitely wasn't waterproof.

"Who's there? Lizzy asked. She sat next to the tub on her dad's shower chair. Her parents were talking at the dining table.

"Lettuce."

"Lettuce who?"

"Lettuce in, it's freezing out." Laughing, Julian ducked his head into the water and kicked his legs, soaking his sister and the bathroom.

"Okay Jules, bath time is officially over!" Julian rinsed off and carefully climbed out of the tub. Lizzy wrapped him up in his Peanuts towel, pulling the terrycloth hood over his wet hair.

"Now it's pajama time! And if you're a good boy, maybe some pudding before you brush your teeth."

"I love pudding! And I love you, Lizzy! You're the best sister in the whole wide world." Lizzy's heart melted.

Subject : Hi !
From : elizamurphyzander@gmail.com
To : hannahabanana99@yahoo.com

Dear Hannah,

22 DAYS! That's when my summer will be over and I'll have to go to middle school! Knowing Walt goes to School of Tomorrow makes me feel a teeny tiny itty bit better.

What am I going to wear on the first day? I don't want to wear something that screams "Loser From New Jersey." I want to look like the cool and confident New York City girl that I'm supposed to be now. Ughhhh!

What are you going to wear? Are you and Amy walking together? Are you going to bring or buy your lunch? The food is still probably unappetizing, right? I mean, isn't all cafeteria food gross? Not as disgusting as the hospital food my dad had but still really bad. I bet you anything that School of Tomorrow's food tastes like rotten eggs or moldy meat or fermented milk.

I miss Ms. Webster and Mr. Scott! Tell them I said Hi! Wait, are they teaching 6th grade?

My mom asked me if I wanted a bra (!!). Cassandra already wears one (!!!). I'll have to think about that. Did you get one yet???

I don't know what's going to happen with my dad. He's falling all the time. I'm scared.

Did you go shopping for school supplies yet? Cassie has this rainbow pen that lets you write in 6 different colors!!! I wish I had a pen like that.

Love 'til the ocean freezes,
Me

P.S. Did you like my birthday card?

Chapter 27

"I see your mom," whispered Lizzy. "She's talking to a lady with a purple hat."

Lizzy and Cassandra were lined up against the blue-tiled wall with the rest of the swim class. Across the pool, a group of parents were gathering on the bleachers to watch this final lesson.

"That's Oliver's mom," Cassandra whispered back.

"Who's Oliver?" Lizzy realized she didn't know anyone's name except for Cassie's. She could have tried harder to make friends with the kids in her swim class. Now it was probably too late.

"Oliver Snyder....in the checkered swim shorts? Over there?"

She looked at the kids in the line. Oliver was the second one on the other end, next to the boy with the goofy goggles.

"Oh, you mean the other teacher's pet?"

"Ha ha. Wait, isn't that your dad?"

Lizzy followed Cassie's gaze to the viewing section. She saw her dad climbing the steps of the bleachers. He grabbed hold of the railing and slowly hoisted himself up, his weaker leg lagging behind. In his other hand he held his cane.

What was he doing here? Lizzy thought, anxiety filling her chest.

"Good afternoon, swimmers!" Ms. Olsen said. "We have some visitors today. Let's impress them with your skill and grace. First, I want to see beautiful dives, then give me two laps of freestyle, followed by two of breaststroke."

She blew her whistle. "Line up, everyone! Let's swim!"

Lizzy tried to forget about her dad and focus instead on diving, not falling, into the pool. After curling her toes, bending her knees, and jumping, she somehow managed to execute a pretty decent dive.

"Good job, Miss Zander!" Lizzy heard Ms. Olsen say as she came up for air. That was the confidence she needed. Transitioning to a crawl, she kicked her feet hard and curved her arms to give her stroke more power.

She got a tiny bit out of sync turning her head to breath but managed to adjust before she hoped anyone noticed. Touching the wall, she ducked under the water until she heard the whistle again.

"Time to switch to breaststroke, people!" Lizzy pushed herself off the wall, bent her knees like a frog, and scooped her arms out in front of her. She dipped her head in and out of the water as she picked up speed. She finished the lesson with flying colors.

"Murphy, I'm so proud of you! You must be part mermaid!" said Lizzy's dad afterwards. The parents had come to the deck to greet their swimmers. Ms. Olsen circulated, shaking hands and dishing out compliments. Lizzy's dad used his cane to stand upright.

"Thanks Dad, but I didn't even know you were coming!" She had wrapped a towel around her shoulders and held her pink swim cap in her hand. "It's like not a big deal."

"We got an invitation in the mail, and I wanted to surprise you," said her dad. "I can't wait to tell Mom and Jules how amazing you were!"

"But isn't it too hot in here for you? Doesn't it make your M.S. worse?" she said, lowering her voice.

"I'm A-Okay, sweetheart. Don't worry about me. It's your day!"

"Hi Mr. Zander!" Cassandra said as she came toward them. Beads of water dotted her brown skin. Her braids were dripping.

"Hi Cassie, nice job today. Now I know what you and Lizzy have been up to all summer!"

"Thanks! Didn't Lizzy look fantastic? She's been practicing her dives."

"You both did great! I'm sure your mother is proud."

"Wait, did your mom leave already?" Lizzy asked, looking around the pool deck.

"Yeah, she's in the middle of a big court case, so she could only stay for the beginning." Lizzy could sense Cassie's disappointment.

"Can I take a photo, girls?" Lizzy and Cassie put their arms around each other and grinned. Lizzy's dad snapped a picture with his iPhone.

"Can I see?" Lizzy said, grabbing her dad's phone to look at the photo.

"Now, what about some celebratory ice cream?"

"Thanks Dad!" said Lizzy.

"Yeah, thanks, Mr. Zander. That's so nice of you."

Reaching into his pocket to retrieve his wallet, Lizzy's father accidentally knocked the cane out of his other hand. His leg collapsed and he fell, hitting the tile floor with a thud.

Ms. Olsen and another parent rushed to help, lifting her dad back up. Someone else found a folding chair and helped him sit down. A few kids stopped talking to stare. Lizzy nearly died of embarrassment.

"Feeling better, sir?" Ms. Olsen asked. Luckily, he wasn't hurt.

"Yes, I'm fine, thanks so much. Just knocked myself off balance a little."

Ms. Olsen nodded and went to collect an abandoned towel on a bench nearby. By then the other students and their parents had wandered off to the locker room or to wait in the Y's lobby. Lizzy's dad handed her a ten-dollar bill.

Ms. Olsen walked back over to them. "Terrific job, girls!" She shook both their hands, one after the other. "Enjoy the rest of your summer!" Lizzy and Cassandra exchanged looks. "Thanks!" they said in unison.

Lizzy's dad stood up and carefully stretched his legs as he held on to the bench.

"Go get your ice cream, mermaids! See you at home." He turned toward the exit, supporting himself with his cane as he stepped forward.

ξ

"I'll have a dish of chocolate almond fudge, please. And she'll have a pralines and cream on a sugar cone," Lizzy said to the teenage girl working at Frosty's.

"Cassie, there's a table!" Cassandra took off running across the shop.

"I can't believe swim class is over!" said Lizzy, handing Cassandra her cone.

"I can't believe Ms. Olsen shook our hands. That was awkward."

"Super awkward."

"You think your dad will get home okay?"

Lizzy hoped her mom wouldn't be mad at her for leaving him at the pool, but he insisted. She took a bite of ice cream and let the crunchy cold sweetness melt in her mouth.

She didn't want to think about her dad right now, so she just nodded instead. "Can I ask you something?" she said to Cassandra.

"Yeah?"

"What happened with Hazel and Dylan? I know you don't want to tell the Secret Club, but can you tell me?" She took another bite. Cassie licked her cone.

Cassandra took a big breath and exhaled dramatically. "Hazel woke up one day and decided she didn't want to be my best friend anymore."

"Because of Dylan?"

"Yup. Dylan Quinn. Best Friend Stealer."

"And?"

"For spring break last year, Dylan was allowed to invite four friends to her beach house. She was obviously going to pick Olivia, Kenya, and Siobhan because the four of them had existed in their own universe ever since Dylan waltzed into school on the first day of fifth grade and acted like she owned the place. They did everything together, they looked alike, had the same hair, and treated the rest of us like garbage."

"They were mean girls?" Lizzy was captivated.

"The Queens of Mean. So when I found out that Hazel, my best friend since first grade, the one who played dress-up with me and celebrated every single birthday since we were six years old, had been invited to be the fourth guest, I was like, well, she'll never go because Dylan was stuck up and full of herself and didn't have a nice bone in her body. Plus, I hadn't been invited. We had a pact, or so I thought."

Cassie paused to bite her cone.

Lizzy's head was spinning. "So, then what happened?"

"Guess!"

"Hazel went?"

"Yup. She fell under Dylan's spell. And did she say a single word to me about it ever?"

"Um, no?"

"She didn't say anything. I had to find out from Zadie who told Carmen who told Alison who told me. Hazel was either too chicken to tell me herself or she decided she liked Dylan better. I mean, she is gorgeous and popular and has the coolest shoes. But we were best friends!"

"When Hazel got back from Dylan's beach house, she didn't talk to you?"

"Not one word. And she started sitting with the four of them at lunch. It was like I never meant anything to her."

"I'm sorry, Cassie. That must hurt so much," said Lizzy. "What happened after the concert? Remember you were starting to tell us?"

"Oh that." She shook her head at the memory. "Well, a bunch of us were standing in front of the school waiting to get picked up when Hazel walked by with Dylan and her clique. When they passed by, I called Dylan's name. When she turned around, I asked her why she wanted to be friends with a girl who still sucked her thumb."

"You actually said that?" Lizzy couldn't hide her surprise.

"I know, it wasn't the best choice, but it's the truth."

"Did Dylan say anything?"

"Nope, they just kept on going."

"Do you think Hazel heard you?"

"I don't know, and I don't care."

"Wow." Once again, that was all Lizzy could think of to say. Cassandra's story left her speechless.

Chapter 28

"Murphy, can we talk to you for a minute?" her dad said in an unusually serious voice. It was after dinner and Julian was in his room playing with his horses and his new red barn.

Her dad was sitting on one side of the couch. Lizzy's mom sat next to him, holding his hand.

"Hi. What's going on?" said Lizzy as she took a seat across from her parents. "You're making me nervous."

"Daddy had an M.R.I. yesterday. You remember what that is, right? The test to look inside his brain."

"I know what an M.R.I. is, Mom," Lizzy said, impatiently. She was rocking in the rocking chair and not looking at her parents' faces. Penny sat on her lap, her paws resting on the arm of the chair. Lizzy scratched her head.

"Well, my doctor told me the results showed the white patches had grown. Do you know what that means?" her dad asked gently.

"That you're getting worse. That's why you keep falling."

"Yes, I think so. M.S. is still a mystery in a lot of ways, but more white patches probably means that my disease is progressing faster. I know how scary it is for you when I am so unsteady and lose my balance. Like the other day coming back from the library and then at the pool."

"But you have your cane...." Lizzy's voice trailed off.

"Sweetheart, Daddy's doctor thinks it would be easier and safer if he used a wheelchair to get around," explained her mom.

Wheelchair. That word made Lizzy think of walk-a-thons for handicapped kids or old people whose bones were so fragile that walking even two steps was impossible. Not her father. He didn't belong in a wheelchair.

"Okay, I understand. Can I go now?" She stood up and stuck her hands in the pockets of her shorts.

"We thought we could talk about how you're feeling about all this. It's a lot to take in. Do you have any questions?" asked her mom. Lizzy looked at her feet.

"I'm fine. Can I please go? I told Julian I would read to him."

"Yes, course. We're here if you want to talk. We love you, Murphy," said her dad. Lizzy bolted out of the living room and threw herself onto her unmade bed.

The tears came hot and fast. She didn't try to stop them. In minutes her pillowcase was soaked. With a runny rose, swollen eyes, and a beet-red face, Lizzy felt like she had been hit by a truck. She didn't dare look in the mirror. Her reflection would probably make her cry even harder.

She found her phone in the jumble of sheets and blankets on her bed.

Hey. She hoped Cassandra was around. She was leaving for the beach early the next morning.

The three dots appeared.

Do you miss me already?!

Just had a talk with my parents

About what?

They told me my dad is getting worse.

He is? Sorry

He's getting a wheelchair.

Oh.

What am I going to do w/out u?!

I'll be home before you know it. Maybe next summer you can come with us.

That would be so fun. You all packed???

Yup.

Don't forget your sunscreen!

I won't. I gotta go. My mom needs me. I'll text you from the car.

OK. Miss you. xoxo

Everything is going to be fine, Lizzy. Have fun. Try to relax!

I'll try. Have fun at the beach. Get a tan for me!

She typed a smiley face.

After a while of feeling sorry for herself, Lizzy got up, blew her nose, brushed her hair, and went to see what Julian was up to. As she walked through the living room, she saw that her parents had gone into their bedroom. She could hear their muffled voices through the door. More grown-up talk.

"Hey Jules, are you still awake?" she announced as she stepped into her brother's room, which was jam-packed with toys, books, and stuffed animals.

"No, I'm sleeping!!!" came the reply, followed by a trail of giggles.

Wearing blue footed pajamas, Julian was lying on his stomach scribbling in a Superman coloring book. Crayons were scattered everywhere. Lizzy snuggled up to him, close enough to smell his toothpaste breath, and smoothed his hair, damp from his bath.

"I think it's past someone's bedtime." She helped Julian back into bed, pulled up his blanket, and handed him Bob the Bunny.

"You said you'd read to me," he said in the sweetest voice.

"Since you asked so nicely. Just one book, then it's light's out." Julian scooched over to make room for his sister. Halfway into *The Snowy Day*, they were both out.

Chapter 29

Lizzy wished she could stretch out these last few weeks of summer like a luscious piece of chocolate taffy (even though it always seemed to get stuck in her teeth).

Without Cassandra, she had to figure out what to do with herself. Swim class was over. The Secret Club wasn't meeting right now. And the weather was terrible.

The blazing sun made the garbage on the sidewalks stink. It was too hot to walk Penny more than half a block, after which time she started panting and pulling the leash back toward the air-conditioned building.

Lizzy spent an hour and a half reading and drawing. Spilling her colored pencils out on her bed, she stared at the empty sheet of paper, waiting for an idea to come to her.

As she looked up, she noticed the photo of Hannah and Amy sitting on her dresser, where it had been all summer long. She decided to draw them. She still missed them.

With a charcoal pencil, she outlined the two figures, their oval heads, round shoulders, arms linked together.

As she detailed their features—Amy's almond-shaped eyes and long shiny hair, Hannah's small nose and round cheeks—her friends began to come to life. She never forgot what Aunt Fiona told her, that she saw the world like an artist.

Sketching in her quiet room, Lizzy thought back to Mount Olive and her life before. Would Hannah and Amy even recognize the Lizzy she had become?

As the time approached noon, Lizzy realized she was hungry. Emerging from her room, she saw her father reading the newspaper in the living room. Instead of his usual place on the couch, he sat in his shiny blue wheelchair, which had a padded seat, thick tires, and needed to be plugged in every night. He had gotten it a few days ago.

"Hi Dad."

"Hey Murphy, how's my girl?"

"I've been drawing. How are you? How do you like your new..." She paused.

"My new wheelchair?"

"Yeah, your new wheelchair."

"Well, it is an adjustment. But I can see how being on wheels will make my life—our lives—easier and less stressful."

"I hope so," Lizzy mumbled.

Her dad could go fast, slow, spin in circles, and stop on a dime by pushing a control knob on the right arm. It took practice: already, he had scraped the paint off the wall by the bathroom, dented the elevator, and almost run over Bob the Bunny, sending Julian into hysterics. Lizzy managed to grab the stuffed toy out of the way at the last second.

The door to their apartment building was also a challenge—it was heavy, and Lizzy's dad had to pull hard on the handle while turning the key—but he was getting the hang of it. Fortunately, there was usually someone passing by who could hold it open for him.

Julian called their father's blue motorized chair "Daddy's Car" and begged for rides. Lizzy was less enthusiastic. She wasn't sure if she would ever get used to the wheelchair. It was big and clunky and totally in the way.

At least her dad wouldn't fall anymore, she reasoned. Then, another thought popped into her head: *Any hope of being a normal family was gone.*

Lizzy hated herself for thinking this way. What did "normal" mean anyway?

"I'm going to finish my drawing," she said, picking up a banana from the fruit bowl on the table.

But when Lizzy got back to her room, she didn't feel like drawing anymore. She decided to do something else.

Searching through her dresser and under her bed, she finally found what she was looking for at the bottom of a drawer where she kept her winter stuff and photo albums: The School of Tomorrow envelope with the smiling globe on the front.

Leaning on the edge of her bed, she opened it. On top, there was a letter.

Dear Sixth Grader:

It is my pleasure to welcome you to School of Tomorrow!

Your teachers and I are excited to meet each one of you and help you get settled for what I know will be a terrific school year.

With your parents, please review the enclosed documents (Student Handbook, Sixth Grade Orientation Schedule, and Calendar of Important Dates). Please also take a few minutes to answer the questions on the yellow sheet of paper. Remember to bring it with you on the first day, Wednesday, September 6.

School begins promptly at 8:25 a.m.

See you then!

Marisol P. Sanchez, Principal

Lizzy scanned the contents of the yellow paper. "Okay, let's see what I have to do here," she said out loud to no one in particular, although Penny, who was sleeping on the floor below, perked up at the sound of her voice and wagged her tail expectantly.

In between taking bites of banana, which was a little too mushy for her liking, she wrote down her answers. She wanted to use her favorite purple pen but decided pencil would be better in case she made a mistake.

MY FULL NAME IS: Eliza Murphy Zander
I LIKE TO BE CALLED: Lizzy
DATE OF BIRTH: November 4, 2007
I LIVE WITH: My mom and dad, Julian (my 3-year-old brother) and Penny (my dog)
I'M LOOKING FORWARD TO: Meeting my teachers and making friends
I WISH: I wasn't the new girl
BOOKS I READ THIS SUMMER: *The Mighty Heart of Sunny St. James, Harry Potter and the Deathly Hallows, Wonder, Island of the Blue Dolphins, The Remarkable Journey of Coyote Sunrise*, and some other ones I can't remember
MY FAVORITE SUBJECTS ARE: Art and English
MY LEAST FAVORITE SUBJECT IS: Gym
FOR FUN, I LIKE TO: Draw, read, and go to the movies and museums, hang out with my friends, swim
SOMETHING I WANT TO TELL MY TEACHERS: I just moved to New York City from Mount Olive, New Jersey
WHEN I GROW UP, MAYBE I WILL: Be an artist or a doctor
FOR BREAKFAST, I ENJOY: Egg and cheese sandwiches
THREE WORDS TO DESCRIBE ME ARE: Tall, red hair, nice

When she finished, Lizzy folded the paper in half and then in half again and stuck it in the pocket of her red backpack, feeling relieved for completing her very first middle school assignment.

Then she stood up, did twenty jumping jacks, picked up the silver mirror on her dresser, and stared at her reflection. Is this what an about-to-be sixth grader looked like?

She studied her clear eyes, framed by strawberry-blond eyelashes and brows, a pointy nose, wavy hair that probably needed a trim, and a sea of freckles covering practically every inch of her skin, which was pink from the sun.

She looked at her slightly crooked teeth and stuck out her tongue. Then she returned the mirror to the top of her dresser, slid into her gold flip-flops, and headed outside.

Her dad had offered to go with her, but Lizzy said she was going to meet up with Cassandra's cousin, which wasn't a total lie. It was possible Walt could be shooting hoops right now because he spent half his life at the court. But he and Lizzy didn't have plans.

The real truth was, she wasn't ready to go out in public with her dad and his wheelchair. What if somebody saw them?

Lizzy

Chapter 30

Lizzy walked over to the basketball courts.

On the way, she stopped at the deli to get something else to eat because the banana wasn't nearly enough. She felt in the pocket of her cut-offs and pulled out four dollars, two quarters, a dime and three pennies, the change from when her mom asked her to pick up dishwasher liquid and lemons at the grocery store the day before.

She ordered an egg and cheese sandwich from Sammy.

"Where's Cassie?" he asked, handing her the sandwich wrapped tightly in white paper.

"Oh, she's away."

"I bet you miss her. You two are joined at the hip." Lizzy was surprised and touched.

"Yeah, I do, but she's coming back soon." Lizzy smiled. She did miss Cassandra. She didn't realize how much until she went away two days ago. Now the week was dragging on without much purpose.

As she was talking to Sammy, Yusef walked in from the back room balancing three cartons of eggs in his arms.

"Hey Yusef!" said Lizzy. She hadn't seen him since he read his poem at the Secret Club meeting.

"Hi Lizzy," he said, stacking the eggs next to the grill.

"How's it going?"

"Pretty good. Just working." Then he got busy with two customers who needed their orders rung up. She felt stupid standing there waiting for him to finish, so she walked out, promising herself she'd come by later.

Lizzy imagined Cassie, looking suntanned in her new pink bikini, attracting attention on the boardwalk. She couldn't help feeling a little envious as she walked down the scorching street, sweat collecting along the sides of her tank top and behind her bare knees, the air almost too thick to breathe.

Approaching the court, she spotted Walt, which wasn't hard to do since he towered over everyone else. Her heart did a little back flip inside her chest.

She watched as he expertly dribbled the ball down the court, easily overpowering the two boys attempting to block him, and made a shot. The ball hit the rim and bounced off. Lizzy looked away.

After a few minutes, someone called for a water break. The six players strolled over to the bench and took turns drinking from a red-and-white thermos. Walt, his face dripping and his dark hair wet with sweat, wiped his forehead with the edge of his brown T-shirt.

"Hey, what's up, Lizzy?" he said. "To what do I owe this distinct pleasure?" Walt had a weird way of putting words together that would probably sound awkward coming out of anyone else's mouth.

"You know, just taking a walk. My dad was driving me crazy, so I needed to escape." Lizzy tried to appear casual.

For the first time, she noticed Walt's eyes. They were light brown with flecks of amber and green. She imagined which pencils she'd use to draw them.

"Cool. Well, I better get back to kicking these boys' butts and taking home the prize." He smiled that Walt smile. "Maybe we could hang out sometime before school starts."

"Uh, sure," was all Lizzy managed to say. As he walked back to his friends, she shouted, "Good luck! Hope you win the prize!"

Could she be any lamer?

Subject : Things
From : elizamurphyzander@gmail.com
To : hannahbanana99@yahoo.com

Hi Hannah:

Yesterday, I walked up to School of Tomorrow just to see how long it would take me (7 minutes, moving kind of fast). I don't know why I did that because it made me super anxious just looking at the old brick building with the stupid globe on the sign. A better name would be School of Yesterday! Plus it has stairs in the front so my dad will never be able to get inside.

I feel kind of weird about my dad's new wheelchair. Maybe because I always hoped he would get better. Like one day he would just wake up and be able to walk like a regular person. The thing is, now, I don't think that's going to happen anymore.

The other thing I wanted to tell you: I hung out a tiny bit with Walt. He's funny and easy to talk to. We're supposed to meet up again before school starts (in TWO WEEKS FROM TODAY!!!).

Cassie gets back from her beach week on Saturday!
Write back soon!!!

LTTOF,
Me

Chapter 31

Lizzy's mom had just arrived home from work after picking Julian up from day care. After taking off her sandals, she was standing at the counter in her bare feet, washing her hands in the sink.

She pulled her hair out of its bun, shaking the auburn strands loose, and splashed water on her face. It had been a long week at her new job. A podcast played in the background.

"What are we having?" Lizzy asked. She sat at the table working on a new drawing, a surprise for Cassie.

Her dad was helping Julian straighten up the living room, which meant the horses, Legos, coloring books, and blocks that had been collecting underneath the coffee table all week needed to go back to the toy chest in his room. Then, and only then, could Julian have his animal crackers.

"We're getting a pizza from Joe's. You're going to have to clear the table so we can set it," said her mom, drying her hands on the checkered dish towel. "Oh, sweetie, there's a piece of mail for you over there."

On top of the pile of bills and catalogs was a picture of fruit in a glass bowl. Lizzy was confused. "Wait, what?" she said out loud. "That's mine!" Turning over the postcard, she recognized Aunt Fiona's handwriting.

Dear Lizzy, My Favorite Niece,

Do you like my postcard? I made it from the drawing you gave me! Remember? I brought it to the copy shop, and they reduced the size and printed it out in color for me. Then I glued it onto an actual postcard! How neat is that? Enjoy the rest of summer! And good luck in your new school. I know you'll be a star. Off to yoga! Say hi to Mom, Dad, Jules and Penny. Miss you like mad! Send me your Halloween costume ideas – and Julian's too!

Your favorite aunt,
Fiona
xoxo

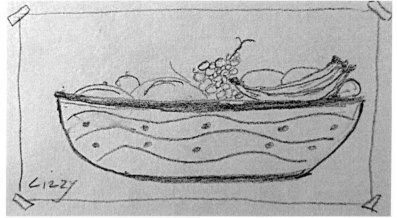

Leave it to Aunt Fiona to think of something so creative and unexpected. Beaming, Lizzy stuck the postcard on the refrigerator with one of the magnets she finally found packed in the last box from the move.

"Daddy's Superman!" shouted Julian, waving his arms in the air. "And this is his magic car!" He climbed onto his father's lap and they spun around in a tight circle, careful not to hit any people, dogs, or stuffed rabbits.

After dinner, Lizzy offered to take Penny for a walk. By then, the rain from earlier had stopped, and the air felt almost fall-like. Slipping into a long-sleeved top and hooking the handle of Penny's leash over her wrist, she headed out.

It was a lively summer night in the city. Restless drivers honked their horns. An ambulance zoomed by toward the hospital, its sirens screaming. A group of older kids hung out in front of the deli, taking videos and playing music at top volume. A couple yelled at each other in Spanish.

As a miniature dachshund approached them, Penny half-heartedly growled and showed her teeth, then, deciding it wasn't worth the trouble, went back to sniffing a tree trunk. Lizzy had remembered to stick a pick-up bag in her pocket, but she hoped she wouldn't need it.

As she rounded the corner of Twentieth Street toward First Avenue, an explosion of fireworks caught her eye. For several seconds, brilliant bursts of color lit up the sky over the East River. Transfixed, Lizzy stared up at the gorgeous display until it was gone.

She had no idea why there were fireworks on a random Friday night in late August, but she couldn't wait to tell Cassandra about it. She smiled to herself as she and Penny turned back toward home.

Suddenly, she heard a rhythmic pounding behind her. It was getting louder and faster. Scared that someone was following her, she and Penny picked up the pace. Two more blocks and they'd be back at her building.

"Lizzy!" She thought she heard her name.

"Lizzy! Wait up!"

Lizzy turned toward the voice and the banging noise. There was Walt, bouncing his basketball on the sidewalk. He wore a navy-blue warm-up jacket over black shorts. His high-tops were red. His smile was from here until forever.

"Oh, it's you, Walt. You kind of scared me," said Lizzy. Was her racing heart fear or something else?

Walt stopped dribbling and held the basketball in his hands. Lizzy noticed how long his fingers were. "My apologies, Lizzy. I didn't mean to freak you out. I just noticed you up ahead walking your dog. You're hard to miss."

They had stopped in front of the diner. Walt leaned down to pet Penny. Lizzy shuffled nervously, shifting her weight from one sandaled foot to the other.

149

"I know. It's the red hair," said Lizzy, twisting a handful around her fingers.

"Lizzy, it's nighttime. Your red hair doesn't glow in the dark! I meant because, like me, you're vertically enhanced."

"Vertically enhanced? Sometimes you talk funny, Walt. I mean, who says stuff like 'vertically enhanced.' Why don't you just say we're both tall?"

"Okay, we're both tall, but I'm taller," he said, standing up super straight to demonstrate. "And since we're both tall and going to the same school, we should get to know each other a little better."

"I like that idea. Can I ask you something?"

"Ask away."

"Cassandra said you used to go to an all-boys school uptown somewhere?"

"Yeah, Wilmington Prep. My dad got laid off in June, and my parents couldn't afford the tuition for me and my brother anymore. And it was too late to apply for financial aid."

"That's terrible. Aren't you upset?"

Walt shrugged his shoulders. "Not really. I hated wearing a jacket and tie every day. Spencer didn't mind the uniform. He's more of a rule follower."

"Does School of Tomorrow have a basketball team?"

"Varsity and junior varsity! I am definitely trying out for varsity. How do you like New York so far? Isn't the city insane?"

"It's really different from my town in New Jersey, but I'm getting used to it."

"Have you been to Central Park?"

"Not yet, but it's supposed to be nice."

"Nice? A bowl of tomato soup is nice. Central Park is spectacular. You have to check it out."

"I should get my dog home. It's past her bedtime," Lizzy said, glancing at Penny, who was lying down at her feet, eyes closed.

"See you later, Lizzy. Come by the courts tomorrow if you want. I'll be practicing my three-pointers."

Chapter 32

The next morning, Lizzy was helping her mom sort the clean laundry in the living room when she heard a beep.

She glanced over at her phone on the table, letting the edges of the yellow bedsheet she was trying to fold drop to the floor. A text from Cassandra!

I'm back!!! Can you meet me??

Her mother looked up from the basket of clothes. "Lizzy, stay focused!" she said with a sharp tone. "The sooner we finish this, the sooner you can get on with your day. Here, add these to your brother's pile." She handed her two T-shirts and a pair of striped socks rolled in a ball.

Lizzy grabbed the pile and put it on the chair with Julian's other clothes. She wanted to respond to Cassandra, but she knew better than to reach for her phone right now.

In the background she could hear her dad pouring food into the dog's dish and the *thwap thwap* of Penny's tail. The teakettle whistled on the stove.

Her phone beeped a second time. Lizzy ignored it until the laundry was folded in neat stacks on the couch.

"We can put everything away after breakfast," said her mom. "Thanks for your help, sweetheart." She turned to Julian, who had come in from the other room carrying Bob the Bunny by the ear.

"Good morning, baby. Are you hungry?"

Lizzy picked up her phone. Cassandra's messages filled the screen.

Hello?

Are you there?

Can you meet?

OMG! Lizzy tapped. *Can't believe you're back! Missed you so much!!!*

OK so can you come? Been waiting forever over here...

Her dad wheeled over to the dining table carrying boxes of cereal on his lap. "Lizzy, get the milk, please. And the orange juice."

Can't leave right now. Meet you at 11:30 at diner?

OK, c u then!

ξ

"I thought you wouldn't be home until tomorrow," said Lizzy after she hugged Cassandra and slid into one of the red vinyl booths, gently dropping her tote bag to the floor by her feet.

A waitress with tattoos covering both her arms and a nose ring handed them menus. Lizzy sipped from her water glass and stared at her friend.

Cassandra's hair was pulled up in a knot on top of her head and fastened with a scrunchie. Her face, a few shades darker since they last saw each other, glowed.

"We had to leave a day early because my mom has this big case at work, and she needs to get ready to go to court on Monday," Cassandra said, playing with the corner of the laminated menu as she talked. "She thought she had more time, but the judge moved the hearing up a week."

Lizzy had no idea what that meant. All she cared about was that her best friend was home at last. "So, what's going on? Tell me everything!" she said.

"It was a boring week. I definitely didn't have as much fun as you had. I couldn't use my phone. Remember, it was a screen-free vacation," Cassandra said, making air quotes with her fingers. "We did watch a little TV, but I couldn't use my cell phone."

"Well, you were at the beach, which is way better than disgustingly hot New York City," said Lizzy. "I almost died of heat stroke."

"Yeah, you're right. And I did get a nice tan, see?" She held up her arm for Lizzy to admire. Lizzy placed her pink freckled arm next to Cassandra's brown one. They smiled. The waitress returned to take their order.

"I hung with Walt a little," Lizzy said as they waited for their food to arrive. "You know he goes to School of Tomorrow, right? It's just kind of weird that you never mentioned that."

Cassandra's mouth shot open. "What? No, he doesn't. He goes to Wilmington Prep uptown. It's sort of my school's brother school. He's gone there ever since kindergarten."

"No, Cassie," said Lizzy, shaking her head. "He goes to my school." Her eyes were wide.

"Is that what he told you? That totally makes no sense." Two grilled-cheese sandwiches, a dish of French fries, a bowl of pickles, and a couple of milkshakes arrived at their table. Cassandra reached for the ketchup and squirted some onto the plate.

"Yes! I don't think he'd make that up if it wasn't true, would he?" said Lizzy. She dipped a fry in the ketchup and popped it in her mouth.

"I'm really surprised my mom didn't say anything." *Maybe Walt didn't want Cassie to know he had to change schools,* Lizzy thought. *Or maybe his mom was embarrassed that they couldn't afford the tuition anymore.* Lizzy decided to let it go.

So, did you and your mom get along on vacation?"

"Yeah, most of the time," said Cassandra. "She let me walk to the beach by myself. It was only a block away from our house, but she made me come back in the afternoon to do schoolwork because I'm behind on my summer assignments. I was supposed to finish them before we went away." She took a long sip of her chocolate milkshake.

"That's so annoying," said Lizzy. "Want some?"

Cassandra bit into the pickle Lizzy handed her and kept talking. "I didn't have a ton to do—just read a book and write a paragraph about it and practice some math equations, which was easy because I'm a whiz at math. I still have one more book to read, a skinny one." The waitress refilled their water glasses.

"I had to do this thing for School of Tomorrow answering a bunch of questions about myself. I probably sounded stupid."

Lizzy paused to take a bite of grilled cheese, which was crunchy and gooey, just the way she liked it. "I don't know what I'm going to wear on the first day. I wish I had a uniform."

"I'm sure your answers were perfect. And I will help you find something. Maybe we can go shopping later. Will your mom let you? Wait, hold on a sec," Cassandra leaned over and wiped a drop of ketchup off Lizzy's cheek. "That's better."

Lizzy grinned. "Thanks." A moment passed. "Did I tell you about my dad?" Lizzy asked softly.

Cassandra's eyebrows shot up. She put her sandwich down. "Is he okay? He's not back in the hospital again, is he?"

"He got a wheelchair." The words sounded strange like they belonged to someone else. Maybe because she had never said them out loud before.

"You texted me about that, remember? Before I left."

155

"Oh, right." Her face felt hot. She took a drink of water to cool down.

"How's it working out? The wheelchair, I mean."

"Good, I guess. He doesn't fall anymore, and he can go really fast."

"Anything else for you today, girls?" the waitress asked, interrupting their conversation.

"I think we're all set, right, Cassie?" She looked at her friend. "Just the check, please." The waitress nodded and walked away.

"It's my treat. Remember, you bought me the nail polish. My dad gave me double my allowance for helping Julian when he cut his head."

"Why are you upset about your dad's wheelchair?"

"I'm not. It's helping him. I hated when he fell down all the time, but..."

"But what?"

"I don't know." Another moment passed. Lizzy drank her milkshake and stared off across the diner. "I just wish things were different sometimes. I can't pretend anymore that there's nothing wrong with my dad."

"Oh. Sorry, Lizzy."

"Never mind, I'm being a baby. Let's talk about something else."

"I almost forgot. I got you something from the beach." Cassandra reached into the front pocket of her shorts and pulled out a tiny pink seashell on a silver chain.

"If you listen really carefully, you can hear the ocean," she said. "Here, let me help you."

Lizzy stood up and turned around, lifting her hair off her neck. Cassandra connected the clasp. "I love it so much!" she said, rubbing the soft shell between her fingers.

"When we're done, do you want to walk over to the basketball courts?"

"To see Walt? Sure," said Cassandra. "But can we stop at the drug store first? I'm all out of strawberry Lip Smackers, and I want to try the root beer one, too!"

"Wait, I have something for you too."

From her bag Lizzy pulled out a green folder with masking tape along the edges. "Sorry, it was kind of tricky to wrap."

"Ooh, I love presents!" Cassandra answered gleefully.

"Open it! But wipe your hands first," said Lizzy. She handed her a napkin.

Carefully tearing the tape, Cassandra lifted up the folder to reveal a sheet of paper from Lizzy's sketch pad transformed with bright shapes and colors.

"What's this? One of your drawings?"

"Yup. I drew it from the photo my dad took of us at the swim thing. See, there we are on the pool deck." Lizzy leaned across the messy table to point to the picture.

"Yeah, that was right before your dad fell."

"I try not to think about that part," said Lizzy. *Why did Cassie have to bring that up now?* she thought. "So, do you like it?"

Cassandra held the paper close to her face and studied every detail.

"Well, it doesn't really look like us," she said finally. "And my bathing suit has different straps."

"Oh."

Lizzy was disappointed. She had worked hard on that.

"If you don't want it, I can hang it on my wall," she said quietly.

An awkward moment went by.

"No, no, sorry! I'm so dumb. Of course I want it. It's great. Really. I'm going to hang it up in my room!"

She placed the drawing back in the folder and stood up. "Come on, let's get out of here!"

Chapter 33

The day Arlo died, Lizzy was in her room unpacking a bag of school supplies she had bought at the stationery store next to Frosty's, the one with the creepy-looking baby dolls in the window that had probably been there since before Lizzy was born. She always thought they were watching her.

When she was little, Lizzy preferred stuffed animals more than dolls—she still had her old teddy bear, Woody—plus, her mother never let her have a Barbie, which was fine because she thought Barbies were stupid and sexist.

At the store, Lizzy picked out five spiral notebooks in red, blue, white, yellow, green, and purple, a packet of folders, a stack of index cards, a box of blue ballpoint pens, six No. 2 pencils and a mini sharpener, and a polka dot pencil case with a zipper down the middle.

She insisted on going by herself. Her mother had left some money on the table before she went to work.

"Lizzy?" Her dad wheeled into her room. The door was ajar.

"Hey, Dad."

"Wow, check out all this good stuff!" he said, admiring the neat pile of supplies on Lizzy's bed. "You're going to be more than ready when school starts."

"Yeah, I guess."

"Listen, I just talked to Mom." He paused. "Arlo died this morning so she's pretty upset. You know how much she loved that cat."

"He did?" said Lizzy, her voice catching in her throat. "That's so sad."

Lizzy felt bad that she never visited Arlo when he was first diagnosed. She could have found the time to take the bus up to Best Friends United. She wasn't all that busy, especially last week when Cassandra was away. Was she a selfish person or just hopelessly pre-occupied with her own life?

She decided to make her mom a card. On the front she sketched Arlo curled up in a ball with his ears pointing up and his little whiskered face peeking out over his front paws.

She filled in his fur with thin lines of orange and black pencil and a hint of dusty pink for his nose. Hearts of different sizes and shades decorated the background.

Inside the card, in her best print, Lizzy wrote:

Dear Mommy,

I'm sorry about Arlo. He was a cool and courageous cat.
I know you will miss him.

Love, Lizzy
Meow, Meow

She put her homemade card in an oversized envelope, licked the flap, and leaned it up against the fruit bowl on the table for her mom to find when she arrived home.

Then she walked down the hall, opened her closet, and stared at the clothes hanging there, minding their own business.

For a least a full minute, she stared, not moving a muscle. But her mind was working overtime. *What if I wear my Levi shorts with the pink-and-white top and my new sneakers?* she thought. *Or, the black leggings with the flowy short-sleeved blouse and my ballerina flats? Or...*

"Lizzy, you are acting crazy!" she heard herself say. "It doesn't matter what you wear! It matters who you are on the inside." Even though she said this out loud, she wasn't sure she believed what she was saying.

Her father called from the kitchen, "Everything alright over there?" He had heard her talking to no one.

"I'm just giving myself a pep talk." But it wasn't working. She closed the closet door and went to text Cassandra.

Hey, we still on?
For what?
Hanging out! Did you forget???
Just messing with you

161

Really?

I can meet soon. Finishing homework. OK if I invite Walt?

Sure. But he's prob busy w basketball

You never know. See you out front in half hour

K

"Dad, I'm going to meet Cassie and Walt. See you later, alligator," Lizzy said. She picked up her tote bag and walked to the door, rubbing extra-strength sunscreen all over her face and arms.

"Where will you be?"

"I don't know, just the usual places. Probably the park or the diner."

"Okay, just stay in the neighborhood."

"Obviously."

Chapter 34

"Did you know there are more rats in New York City than humans?" Walt announced as they stood at the Union Square bus stop waiting for the M1. It was another hot, humid, and disgusting August afternoon.

For the third time, Lizzy checked that her MetroCard was safely in the pocket of her bag and her phone was turned up. Her heart was beating fast. *I can't believe I'm doing this,* she thought.

"OMG, that is the grossest thing I have ever heard," said Cassandra. "Where do you come up with this stuff, Walt?"

"Um, it's called the Internet, Cassie. Ever heard of it?"

"No never, what's that?" she said, her voice thick with sarcasm.

"Guys, I think the bus is coming," said Lizzy, squinting down the street. Sure enough, a blue city bus roared in their direction and stopped in front of Food Emporium.

Cassandra tried to get on the bus, but the driver held up his hand. "Just a minute, please," he told her. She stepped back and joined Lizzy and Walt and a cluster of other people waiting to board. *You don't have to get on,* Lizzy told herself.

Just then, a high-pitched beeping noise interrupted her inner dialogue. Lizzy looked up to see a metal ramp unfolding. Then a woman in an electric wheelchair rolled off and zoomed past them along the sidewalk.

Lizzy couldn't help thinking about her dad. It was good that wheelchairs could go on buses, but wouldn't everyone be staring at him and annoyed that he slowed them down?

The ramp folded up again, and the driver waved the riders on. Lizzy followed her friends to the row of seats in the way-back. The bus was filling up with passengers.

"Let's take a photo!" said Cassandra. "You do it, Walt. You have the longest arms! Use my phone. It has a better camera." She handed Walt her phone with the sparkly purple case.

"Come on, Lizzy, what are you looking at?" Lizzy turned from the window and slid over to join the others. She felt anxious. "I'm not sure this is such a good idea," she said.

"You mean, the photo? Because your hair's a mess?" asked Cassandra. "Don't worry, no one cares!"

"I care," joked Walt. "Because your hair needs to look as perfect as mine." He ran his free hand through his shiny brown locks.

"No, this trip to Central Park," Lizzy said, touching her head self-consciously. *It probably was a mess.* "It's kind of far, don't you think?" They had decided on the spur-of-the-moment to take the bus to the park because Lizzy hadn't been there yet. Actually, it was Walt's idea. He loved Central Park.

Lizzy knew her parents would kill her if they found out she took the bus all the way to Seventy-second Street without their permission. Or at least ground her for the rest of her life. *Why had she agreed to such a crazy plan?*

"Can we just take the photo, please?" urged Cassandra. "Lizzy, you get on the other side. I'll be in the middle because I'm the shortest."

They squished together. Walt held Cassie's phone, lifting it up until they were all in the frame. "Say cheese!"

The bus lurched to a stop at Nineteenth Street. A woman with blond hair and her pig-tailed toddler, who was about Julian's age, settled into the seats in front of them. The little girl was singing "The Wheels on the Bus" at top volume.

"Oh, I love that song," said Cassandra. *"The wheels on the bus go round and round, round and round, round and round..."* The girl turned around and smiled excitedly.

"So, who wants to know more fascinating facts about rats?" said Walt.

"Next stop, Twenty-third Street," announced the driver.

"Absolutely no one. You're making me want to barf," said Cassandra, looking up from her phone. "These photos are so cute. Look, Lizzy!"

"How many more stops?" Lizzy blurted out.

"A lot," said Walt. "Central Park is way uptown. But it will be worth the trip. First, we should go to the fountain, then we can hang out in Sheepshead Meadow. And, we have to get hot dogs, of course!"

"Hot dogs are filled with all kinds of nasty stuff," said Cassandra. "Probably rat meat, too."

"Who's being gross now, Cassie? Huh?" said Walt.

The bus slowed down. Lizzy stood up. Her head was spinning.

"What's wrong?" asked Cassandra.

"I have to go," she said suddenly. "I'll see you guys later. Have fun at Central Park. Sorry."

She hopped off the bus at the next stop and turned back toward home, walking so fast that one of her flip-flops slipped off in the middle of the street and she had to dash back to retrieve it.

She imagined what Cassie and Walt were saying about her right now—probably calling her a goody-goody. She wished she had the courage to be more adventurous, but maybe staying close to home wasn't such a bad thing.

Her phone beeped. A text from Cassandra.

Seriously?!?!? Ur such a baby!!!

She tossed her phone back in her bag without responding.

Subject: Good Luck, etc.
From: elizamurphyzander@gmail.com
To: hannahbanana99@yahoo.com, amyyvonnekim@gmail.com

Dear Hannah and Amy,

I'm writing to both of you at the same time to say: GOOD LUCK on the first day at Edison Middle School! Stay away from Jilly Sinclair and Tiffany Thomas, unless they magically became nice over the summer. Maybe they moved away from Mount Olive! Maybe they're too cool for middle school.

Are you nervous? It's a way bigger school but at least you'll know all the kids from Lincoln and you'll have each other. I hope you get some of the same classes and can sit together at lunch! Are you going to join band, Hannah? And what about soccer, Amy? I miss you both so much. I wish we were walking into town right now talking and laughing at one of your dumb jokes, Hannah. Like why is 6 afraid of 7? Because 7 8 9!!!! Hahahahahaha!

I am definitely NOT looking forward to School of Tomorrow. I am SO nervous I can't even write about it here. I may throw up on my mom's computer.

So, I had this thing with Cassie and Walt earlier. We were supposed to go to Central Park, but I chickened out and got off the bus and went home. Now I feel stupid. It probably would have been really fun, and I ruined everything. Now they are mad at me.

I told my dad I would play Scrabble with him. He just bought this ginormous board that spins around from Amazon. Let me know how day #1 goes!!!!

LTTOF
Me

Later, after Lizzy had helped set the table for dinner, her phone rang. "Be right back," she said to her mom, who washing lettuce at the sink. She grabbed her phone from the counter and dashed into her room, closing the door behind her.

"Hello?" she said, reclining on her unmade bed.

"Hi, it's me," said Cassandra.

"I know."

She could hear Cassandra breathing on the other end.

"If you're calling to yell at me about before, don't bother," said Lizzy. "I know I messed up."

"I'm not."

"Okay."

"Sorry I called you a baby," said Cassandra.

"Sorry I freaked out. Walt probably thinks I'm a total weirdo."

"No, he doesn't. He was just worried you were sick or something."

"Oh. Well, I'm not. I just...

"I know. You didn't feel comfortable disobeying your parents. I get that. I would have gotten in a ton of trouble if my mom found out."

"Yeah, probably," said Lizzy, squeezing a pillow as she talked. "So how was Central Park?"

"It was alright, but we didn't even stay that long. Walt had to get home to see his grandmother. We did get hot dogs, and they were actually pretty tasty."

"Even with the rat meat?"

"Yup! And lots of mustard!" They laughed.

Suddenly, the doorknob turned, and Julian barged in. From her spot on the bed, Lizzy saw him walk toward her, a Band-Aid covering one tanned knee and his shoelaces untied.

"Ever heard of knocking? Can't you see I'm on the phone?" she said, annoyed. "Sorry, Cassie, hold on a sec." She gave her brother an expectant look. "What?"

"Mommy said dinner in five minutes and wash your hands." Then he skipped out, leaving the door open. "Tie your shoes, Jules," Lizzy yelled after him. "You're going to trip!"

She put the phone back to her ear. "I actually have to go. Dinner time."

"Yeah, I heard. Text me after. Maybe we can meet up."

"I will. Wait, should I text Walt?"

"Why?"

"About before, the bus?" Lizzy said, lowering her voice. She didn't want her parents to hear.

"If you want, but I really wouldn't worry about it."

"Okay. I'll text you later."

"Ta-ta!" said Cassandra in her English accent. Smiling, Lizzy rolled off her bed, scrunched her hair, and walked into the kitchen. "Something smells delicious!" she said, kissing her mom on the cheek.

Chapter 35

Labor Day weekend, the official end of summer, was only two days from now. As her parents organized a potluck picnic in the park across Third Avenue, Lizzy felt unsettled.

She didn't want these wide-open days—days where she could do anything she wanted, or nothing at all—to fade away. She wanted to grab hold of the last licks of summer and never let go.

As anxious as Lizzy was to start at her new school, she was also worried about Cassandra. What would happen when they settled into their separate schools? What if what they shared wasn't real after all? What if Cassie forgot all about her?

No matter how many pep talks she gave herself or how many times her parents told her they were proud of her, Lizzy couldn't imagine actually walking into School of Tomorrow on Wednesday.

She thought back to the end of June when her world turned upside down. She was scared then, too, as she tried to figure out her place in New York City, in a family that wasn't quite like other families.

Now, two-and-a-half months later, she was still a red-headed freckle face who loved to draw and play with her little brother and hang out with her friends.

But something inside her had changed.

169

ξ

"Hold still, I don't want to mess up."

Cassandra was painting Lizzy's nails. Facing each other, they sat cross-legged on the grass in McLean Park. It was the day before the first day. Lizzy fanned her hands out in front of her, while Cassandra expertly applied the polish.

"This is the perfect color for you, Lizzy. It's not too wimpy or too wild." She dipped the brush in the bottle and lifted it back out. A drop of grayish-pink polish fell onto Lizzy's knuckle.

"Oops," Cassandra said she wiped if off with a cotton ball soaked in nail polish remover. "Sorry about that."

For a few minutes, neither talked. They were both lost in their own thoughts. Lizzy felt sad, nervous, and happy all at the same time.

In the background, kids laughed as they played on the swings and climbed the jungle gym. A Mister Softee truck, parked across the street, played its jolly tune.

Cassandra looked into Lizzy's face. "You know, you really have cute freckles. I bet not a single person at School of Tomorrow will have such cute freckles and such cool nails!"

"Thanks, Cassie," Lizzy said. "I wish I had your gorgeous skin. It's like coffee ice cream."

"More like milk chocolate, after being in the sun all summer." Then in her fake English accent: "You burn, and I tan. That's why we're a good team." Lizzy threw her head back and laughed.

"Stop moving, I'm almost finished."

"Stop cracking me up!"

"Sorry, I can't help it. Okay, last coat on your pinkie." She gently moved the brush to cover Lizzy's littlest finger. "Tada! All done! Now do this." Cassandra flapped her hands in the hot air.

"I love them! Thanks so much!" said Lizzy. She waved her painted fingers up and down and all around. "So, is your uniform ready to go?"

"Yup, my mom washed my skirt and shirt and hung them in the closet. I just need to figure out what earrings to wear and what shoes. I can't wait to see what Dylan Quinn decides to put on her stupid feet."

"If I were you, I'd stay away from Dylan. What about Hazel? How do you feel about seeing her?"

"I don't know. It'll probably be weird. I miss her sometimes. It hurts that she chose Dylan instead of me, but I'm over it, mostly."

Lizzy smiled. "You should think about trying out for the play. If you're really going to be a movie star, you need lots of practice! Greystone has a middle school play, right?"

"Yeah, maybe I will. I want to join Math Club too. All the nice girls are in Math Club."

"You're so lucky you know everyone at your school. I don't know anyone!"

"Except Walt."

"He finally told you?"

"No, my mom did."

"Oh. Walt isn't even in our grade so who knows if I'll see him. But we are walking together tomorrow. I texted him."

"Good for you! Walt's a great guy."

Lizzy nodded. "I just can't imagine going up to strange kids and saying, 'Hi, I'm Lizzy, will you be my friend?' I'd rather eat eyeballs.'"

"Just be yourself, Lizzy. You have such a big heart. Everyone will see that."

They were quiet for a moment. Lizzy crossed and uncrossed her legs. The grass tickled the backs of her knees. Cassandra looked down at her hands and licked her lips. A dog barked.

"I wish we could go to school together. Wouldn't that be so great?" Lizzy said. She looked over at Cassandra.

"I'd love that. And you'd definitely rock the Greystone skirt!"

Tears burned behind Lizzy's eyes. She squeezed them shut and took a deep breath. There was no way she was going to let herself cry.

"Are they dry yet?" she asked, holding out her hands. With the tip of her finger, which was painted the very same color, she tapped one of Lizzy's nails. "Yup, all dry!"

The girls stood up and brushed off their shorts.

"Want to go to Sammy's?" asked Cassandra.

"Definitely."

Linking arms, they strolled toward their favorite deli. All around, the sounds of the city—horns honking, sirens blaring, cars and buses whooshing by—created a kind of noisy symphony. Lizzy felt right at home.

"Cassie?"

"Yeah?"

"Remember our first swim class?"

"Duh! Of course. That's where it all began. The Lizzy and Cassandra story!"

"It feels like a thousand years ago."

"A million."

"It's been an amazing summer, that's for sure," Lizzy said. "Thanks for being there. I would never have survived without you."

"Hello? Isn't that what best friends are for?"

"One hundred percent!" Lizzy paused. "Do you think we'll always be friends?"

Cassandra's C-shaped earrings caught the sun as she turned her head to look at Lizzy. She smiled with all her teeth.

"At least until the ocean freezes."

Acknowledgements

Thank you to everyone in my life who believed in me, made me laugh, and gave me the strength I needed to persevere through countless revisions, rejections, and doubts. Without you, I wouldn't have had the courage to write this book and launch it out into the world.

Thanks to my wonderful friends, family, colleagues, teachers, librarians, bookstore employees, and fellow writers who helped me along the way. Special gratitude to Jerry Bartell, Cindy Brogan, Abby Formella, Natasha Goldberg, Anne Marie O'Connor, Bryan Oettel, Anne Phinney, Mary Anne Sacco, Sarah Segal, Marvin Terban, Peternelle van Arsdale, Julie Walsh, Maureen Walten, my late mother-in-law Heike Fenton, The New York Society Library, the Society for Children's Book Writers and Illustrators, and Reflections Center for Conscious Living & Yoga.

Boundless appreciation to Lisa Myers, a Vermont-based visual artist and longtime family friend, for the most spectacular cover art, Aoife Leonard for the terrific cover design, and Emily Hainsworth for her editorial expertise. Shout-outs to the insightful and enthusiastic fifth graders in Ms. Dibble and Ms. Wheatley's classes at The Chapin School, to the book-loving members of Chapin's Mock Newbery Club, and to my amazing nieces, Hazel and Chloe Clemans Shapiro.

I am ever grateful to my mother, Paula A. Roy, for raising me to love words and for fiercely championing this book and all of my creative endeavors, and to my twin sister, Shantih Elizabeth Clemans, for absolutely everything, including the beautiful interior illustrations, which she and Chloe created together, and for her assistance, however accidental, with the book's title. I'd be lost without you. LTTOF.

Until the Ocean Freezes was inspired by my husband, Marc Fenton, whose multiple sclerosis is no match for his insatiable zest for life, and our two children, Zoe and Lucas Fenton, who are now accomplished, passionate, and kind young adults. Thank you for allowing me to borrow from your lives to help tell Lizzy's story and for making me incredibly proud. I love you and appreciate your support more than you will ever know.

© Marc Fenton

A professional writer and editor for many years, Alida Durham Clemans decided in 2018 to follow her heart and pursue a career as a children's author. She grew up in Westfield, New Jersey, and holds a degree in English and journalism from the State University of New York at Albany. The mother of two, Alida lives in New York City with her husband and a scruffy rescue dog. When she's not writing kid lit, she works as a writer for an independent school. *Until the Ocean Freezes* is her debut novel. Visit alidadurhamclemans.com.

Made in the USA
Monee, IL
04 March 2020

22475360R00106